You can
worked through your hatred of this man.

That's not going to happen! He tried to ruin me!

Suddenly everything grew dark. The gold light disappeared. Rachel gasped, then coughed violently.

Someone was kneeling at her side, his hand gripping her shoulder. He was screaming for a medic.

She continued to gasp, forcing air into her lungs. No more smoke! She was alive!

Mind barely functioning, Rachel heard the man calling for help once again. He sounded desperate. Afraid for her. Then, as consciousness grew, Rachel felt a shock wave. The man at her side was Captain Tyler Hamilton. Tyler Hamilton, who hated her as much as she hated him.

Groaning, Rachel couldn't handle the emotional tsunami that rolled through her. She blacked out. The last thing she felt was his protective hand on her shoulder. He was the last man on earth that she ever wanted to touch her.

* * *

Dear Reader,

I'm very excited about this book! Why? Because for those who love Morgan's Mercenaries, you need to know that the first-born child of Noah and Kit Trayhern (*A Question of Honor,* May 1989), Melody Sue Rachel Trayhern, is featured in this book!

Rachel is a captain in the U.S. Army and she flies the vaunted Apache helicopter gunship. Rachel almost didn't become a graduate of the Army Apache school because one of the flight instructors, Ty Hamilton, tried to wash her out. In the end, Captain Hamilton was found to be prejudiced toward Rachel simply because she was a woman. He was kicked out as an instructor and Rachel was allowed to complete her training with flying colors.

Now, five years later, Rachel is with the all-women Black Jaguar Apache squadron at a forward CIA base on the Afghanistan-Pakistan border. She loves her job as a combat pilot. When the Taliban attack just as she has landed her Apache at the base, Rachel nearly loses her life. And the man who ends up rescuing her is her old enemy—Captain Ty Hamilton. Join me to see the battle between love and hate as it plays out on the battlefields of Afghanistan.

Warmly,

Lindsay McKenna

www.lindsaymckenna.com

LINDSAY McKENNA

His Duty to Protect

ROMANTIC
SUSPENSE

Recycling programs
for this product may
not exist in your area.

ISBN-13: 978-0-373-27761-2

HIS DUTY TO PROTECT

Copyright © 2012 by Lindsay McKenna

Books by Lindsay McKenna

Harlequin Romantic Suspense
**His Duty to Protect* #1691

Silhouette Romantic Suspense
Love Me Before Dawn #44
†*Protecting His Own* #1185
Mission: Christmas #1535
    "The Christmas Wild Bunch"
**His Woman in Command* #1599
**Operation: Forbidden* #1647

Silhouette Nocturne
Unforgiven #1
Dark Truth #20
The Quest #33
Time Raiders: The Seeker #69
Reunion #85
The Adversary #87
Guardian #89

†Morgan's Mercenaries: Ultimate
**Black Jaguar Squadron
*Warriors for the Light

HQN Books
Enemy Mine
Silent Witness
Beyond the Limit
Heart of the Storm
Dangerous Prey
Shadows from the Past
Deadly Identity
Deadly Silence
The Last Cowboy

Other titles by this author
available in ebook format

LINDSAY McKENNA

As a writer, Lindsay McKenna feels that telling a story is a way to share how she sees the world. Love is the greatest healer of all, and the books she creates are parables that underline this belief. Working with flower essences, another gentle healer, she devotes part of her life to the world of nature to help ease people's suffering. She knows that the right words can heal and that creation of a story can be catalytic to a person's life. And in some way she hopes that her books may educate and lift the reader in a positive manner. She can be reached at www.lindsaymckenna.com or www.medicinegarden.com.

On August 6, 2011, thirty brave men and a dog from the military were shot down while flying in a CH-47 in Afghanistan. I want to honor them and their courageous families. They are truly heroes and paid the ultimate sacrifice for our freedom. My prayers for each family who has lost so much. Bless them all.

Chapter 1

Captain Rachel Trayhern was five steps away from Bravo Base Operations and the control tower when the first Taliban grenade struck the tarmac.

The hot August sun beat down upon her, and their mission had just ended.

A sudden disruption made her flinch, and she whirled around at the hollow "thump" sound. Panic raced through her as she anticipated the fall. Lieutenant Susan Cameron, her copilot, had already gone inside to file their Apache gunship flight report. At least she might be safe.

The enemy grenade landed squarely on her helicopter. The ensuing explosion sent booming shock waves rippling across the landing area. Cheating death once more, the crew that was coming to hitch the Apache up with a motorized cart drove in the other direction. Fire flew toward the sky. Metal erupted and became deadly shrapnel in every direction. Thick, black smoke rolled outward and upward.

A second, third and fourth grenade popped into the sky. Rachel hit the asphalt hard, her helmet bag flying out of her hand. The August sky had been clear blue. Now, as the well-aimed grenade launchers hit the second Apache and a CH-47 Chinook that had landed a few minutes earlier, the whole airport was under siege. *Attack!*

Gasping, Rachel kept her hands over her head. Her helmet bag lay nearby but not close enough. The smoke was thick and choking. She heard the surprised cries of men as the attack continued. Return fire began. Bravo Base was one of the most forward CIA operations in Afghanistan, not more than fifteen miles from the line between this country and Pakistan. And it was always a target of the Taliban.

Crawling to try and find some kind of protection, Rachel heard another *thunk* and knew the enemy had launched yet another grenade. She was out in the open and completely vulnerable. A piece of shrapnel could kill her as easily as a grenade exploding nearby. More shock waves rolled across the air facility. Shrieks of wounded began to fill the air.

Oh, God, let me get out of this alive. The Apaches roared and burned, creating smoke so thick she couldn't see one foot in any direction. Rachel heard the pounding of feet across the tarmac. Orders were screamed above the devastating attack. She felt strangled, helpless. Her brown hair fell loose from its knot, and tears ran down her face as she continued to crawl blindly along the edge of the tarmac. So far, Ops wasn't hit, but she knew the Taliban would try and take it out. She was in real danger.

With return fire of heavy artillery in full force, thumping sounds filled the smoke-clogged air. Special Forces had to be heading for the edge of the base to engage the Taliban. Bravo was surrounded by two ten-foot tall walls with razor-blade sharp concertina wire on top. Somehow, the Taliban had gotten close enough to inflict major damage. The heavy chutter of machine gun fire began in an attempt to ward off the Taliban located at the end of the runway.

Hacking and choking, Rachel crawled swiftly away from the control tower. Her elbows and knees smarted with pain, the asphalt hard on them. Her mind spun with shock over the violent attack. Somehow, she managed to scramble off the tarmac and into the weeds and dirt. She was a good fifty feet away from the tower, which was an obvious target. She worried for her copilot, Susan, whom she hoped had escaped in time.

A hot, black cloud of smoke overtook her. Burying her head in the grass, Rachel could barely breathe. She felt as if she were going to die. As she continued to crawl, blind and constantly coughing, she knew her only way to live was to escape the attack. The roar of the burning helos, the return fire from heavy machine guns reverberated against her unshielded eardrums. Her strength began to dissolve. She was barely getting any oxygen, so she thrust her face down into the weeds, the only place with clean air. Fire sucked and ate up oxygen. Heat from the flames rose.

The wind shifted toward her, a bad sign. Pushing forward, her flight boots digging into the hard Afghan soil, Rachel felt the small rocks and stouter weeds poking into the chest and belly of her green flight suit. She thrust out her hand, fingers like claws digging into

the resisting earth. It rarely rained in August at eight
thousand feet. The land was hard and unyielding.

No! I can't die! Rachel gasped like a fish out of
water, saliva drooled from her mouth as she tried to
suck up the life-giving air. *Oh, God, don't let me die
like this!* Her vision began to gray. More smoke rolled
toward her, hot and stealing her oxygen. The breeze
across the mountains where the base was located was
constant. Now it blew toward where she tried to crawl.

Her senses dulled and tears ran down her face.
Trying with all her might to escape the smoke, she
began to sob. At thirty years old, she had her whole life
ahead of her. And even though she'd been an Apache
gunship pilot for the last five years, she'd never thought
that she'd die crawling across the ground.

Weakened, she lay still for a moment, fighting to get
her consciousness back. The smoke was an oxygen-
sucking monster. The heavy *chut, chut, chut* of machine guns spitting out their bullets became distant.
The flames and roaring fire sounds lessened, too. Her
aching ears seemed filled with cotton, erasing all the
noise that had pounded relentlessly seconds earlier.
Rachel collapsed, her face pressed to the ground, small
rocks biting into her cheekbone. Even that pain seemed
to float away. She was losing consciousness because she
couldn't get enough air into her lungs. No matter what
she did, she no longer had the strength to pull herself
forward. The last thought she had was that after the
fires were put out, they'd find her body in the weeds.

It was an ignominious end, Rachel decided. She
was a combat pilot. A damn good one. She'd battled
through Apache flight school and nearly got kicked
out thanks to Captain Tyler Hamilton, who hated her.
And yet, she'd fought back and remained to graduate.

Shutting her eyes, Rachel thought of her family. Her father, Noah Trayhern, danced before her closed eyes, his smile making her feel better. And her mother, Kit, who was a police detective, had a sharp and alert gaze. Praying, her lips moving, Rachel didn't want her parents to hear from the Army that she'd died of smoke inhalation on a barren, godforsaken mountaintop in Afghanistan.

As her world grayed, her body went slack and consciousness receded. Darkness was complete.

And then Rachel felt someone standing at her side. She couldn't see who it was, but she felt love radiating from this being.

Welcome, Rachel, the being said to her. *You are all right now. You're here to review your life. Are you ready?*

This had to be a dream. There was no voice she could hear. But she could feel the words. Confused, afraid, she looked around. Everything was a bright white light, but not so bright as to make her squint. Finally, she said mentally, *I guess I am ready....*

She began to see the moment when she was conceived. Her mother was very young, very beautiful. Her father was in the Coast Guard, a commander of a cruiser. The love they had for one another overwhelmed Rachel. Her heart opened powerfully.

You were brought into this world with love, a voice said.

Rachel felt hot tears come to her eyes. She loved her family so much! Her given name was Melody Sue Rachel Trayhern. She laughed when she saw herself as a ten-year-old girl talking to her mother, stubbornly telling her mother that she hated the name, Melody Sue. She wanted to be called Rachel, her middle name, because that was her grandmother's name. And Rachel fiercely loved the elder. She saw her mother smile and laugh. From that point on, everyone called her Rachel.

Everything moved swiftly for Rachel as she reviewed her life. She saw four more sisters born to her parents. She was the oldest. And they'd had a very happy childhood. Rachel, the pathfinder for the family, as her father referred to her, wanted to go into the military. She'd been allowed into West Point and had been one of the top ten officers to graduate from that military academy. Rachel's gut tightened as she saw her orders were for Fort Rucker, Alabama, the flight school. She had dreamed of being a pilot, of flying, all her life. Her father told her that flying was in the blood of the Trayherns. Rachel remembered her powerful reaction to that information.

Rachel felt her heart slam shut with pain. She saw her first days at the Apache flight school. Her anger rose as she saw her instructor, Captain Tyler Hamilton. He stood in front of her company, arrogant, a real bastard, who hated women on the same tarmac with him. And he'd singled out Rachel because she was doing better than the other men learning to fly the Apache helicopter. More rage rose as she watched Hamilton plot her demise. Sheer hatred, that's what flowed through her. This son of a bitch was going to flunk her out of school. The dream of flying was dying.

Rachel, the voice said gently. *Until you make peace with this man you cannot leave.*

Confused, Rachel looked around. She was surrounded in a white-and-gold glowing fog. How she wished again she could see who owned this voice.

That way she could explain face-to-face that she could never forgive Hamilton. He tried to ruin her.

He'd said the Trayhern family was always trying to get what they didn't deserve. Well, that wasn't true. She'd worked damned hard to get her wings at Fort Rucker. She was a good pilot. That bastard wouldn't take her dream away. The Trayhern family served its country with pride and honor. No way would she stand there and let him kick her out.

Because of your ongoing hatred, you must go back and work through this with him.

Before Rachel could say a thing, she felt a powerful, whirling sensation, as if she were in a funnel, spinning around and around. Then she fell and everything grew dark. The gold light disappeared, and the blanket of love dissolved. Suddenly, it was as if an anvil were sitting on her chest. She gasped and coughed violently.

Her eyes flew open. The sunlight nearly blinded her, and she found herself on her back in the dirt and grass. Someone was kneeling at her side, gripping her shoulder. He was looking into her eyes, panic in his. His mouth opened and he raised his head, screaming for a medic.

Rachel felt the strong touch of his hand, saw the care and fear in his blue eyes. Her mind refused to work properly. She continued to gasp, grabbing her chest as if to force air into her lungs. Weapons continued to fire in the distance, and she heard men and women calling out orders. The sky. Staring up at the blue sky, Rachel blinked as her chest heaved. No more smoke! The smoke had moved. She was alive. Alive!

Mind barely functioning, Rachel heard the man at her side calling for help once again. He sounded desperate. Afraid. For her? And then as her consciousness grew, Rachel felt a shock wave of another kind roll through her. This one took her breath away. The man at her side was Captain Tyler Hamilton, the instructor pilot who had almost gotten her flunked out of Apache flight school. What the *hell* was he doing on her base? Rachel's mind shorted out, and she struggled to make sense of what was happening. Was this a nightmare?

Groaning, Rachel couldn't handle the emotional tsunami, and she blacked out. The last thing she felt was his protective hand on her shoulder. He was the last man on earth who she ever wanted to touch her.

"Rachel? Rachel, wake up...."

A woman's urgent voice filtered through her gray consciousness. Rachel frowned. There was a hand on her other shoulder now, a woman's hand. She fought to wake.

"Hey, Cousin. It's Emma. You're all right. You're going to live. Come on, wake up."

Cousin? Her mind was frayed. Rachel tried hard to surface. The hand on her shoulder was gentle and soothing, as if to remind her she was alive. Was she? Emma? Yes, she knew Emma. Emma had just married Khalid Shaheen, an Afghan officer in the U.S. Army. He flew the Apache. Rachel clung to this bit of information. If she didn't, it would leave. Desperately, she forced herself to remember. In July, everyone had gotten leave to fly back to San Francisco. Emma and Khalid had been married there in Golden Gate Park. The whole Trayhern clan had attended, including patriarch Morgan and his beloved wife Laura, Noah and Kit, and Emma's parents, Alyssa and Clay, were there to celebrate the wedding.

"Rachel? You're doing fine, you're coming back," Emma whispered near her ear. "You're here at Bravo

Camp. You're in the dispensary. You're going to be okay...."

Emma's husky voice was like a beacon. She fiercely loved Emma. And Rachel had cried when the Army had released her cousin from duty. Emma had sustained nerve damage to her left hand after being captured by the Taliban. And without her feeling in that hand, she wasn't permitted by the U.S. Army to fly her beloved Apache. But Emma was strong, and her fiancé had given her a CH-47, which his family had bought, to fly instead. Emma had come back married, and still worked out of Bravo Base with Khalid. She flew nearly every day as a civilian contractor hired by Khalid's family to deliver books and educational supplies to villages along the Afghan border. Now, Emma was here with her. Emma!

Though it felt as if bricks were weighted upon her eyes, she forced them open. Rachel saw fuzziness at first. But Emma's red hair, her face and those dancing green eyes slowly came into focus in front of her.

Emma smiled and brushed some hair away from Rachel's scrunched brow. "Hey, Cuz, welcome back to the land of the living. How are you doing?"

Rachel lifted her hand and felt an oxygen mask over her nose and mouth. The air tasted wonderful! She tried to reorient. Emma continued to gently rub her shoulder as if to coax her back to full consciousness. As she closed her eyes, the attack on the base roared back at her. The noise, the danger, the carnage. Her Apache helo had been destroyed. The thick, black smoke rolling across her and cheating her of oxygen came next.

"Come on, open your eyes, Rachel."

She obeyed and saw Emma in her dark green flight suit standing beside her. She was smiling down at her, relief clearly written in her expression. "Hey, you had me scared there for a while."

Groaning, Rachel was now aware of the frantic activity in the dispensary. There were orderlies, nurses and doctors rushing everywhere. Of course, she thought, we're under attack…people are hurt…maybe dead.…

Patting her shoulder, Emma gave a sigh of relief. "You're okay, Rachel. The dude who brought you in said you'd nearly suffocated in that smoke. Thanks to him, you're alive and not dead."

Mind spinning, Rachel took off the oxygen mask. Her strength had returned. She was no longer weakened as before. Still dazed, she struggled on the gurney. Emma slid her arm around her shoulders and helped Rachel sit up.

"Hang on," Emma said, "and I'll raise this thing." She leaned down.

Rachel felt the gurney move upward to support her back. "Thanks," she rasped, touching her throat. It felt raw and hot.

Emma straightened and smiled. "How are you feeling?"

"Like I've scalded the inside of my throat," Rachel whispered.

"Here, drink some water." Emma handed her a glass.

Though her hands trembled, Rachel took it. The water tasted wonderful. The cool fluid soothed the pain. "Thanks," she said, her voice sandpapery-sounding even to her.

Taking the glass, Emma nodded. "More?"

"No." Rachel looked around to get her bearings. She'd been here at Bravo for three months. Never had she been inside the small clinic before. A number of medical people were moving and speaking quickly to one another as more injured were brought into the facility. She turned back to Emma.

"I didn't know you were here. I thought you were out flying today."

Nodding, Emma said, "I was. But I'd just landed after the Taliban attack began. Luckily, I was at the other end of the landing strip, so our helo wasn't blown away."

"God, it's awful," Rachel muttered. She pulled her legs off the gurney and allowed them to hang. Looking down, she noticed her uniform was stained with dirt and weeds. Rachel scowled. "I thought I was going to die, Emma. That damned smoke followed me like a good friend. I was in the wrong place at the wrong time…."

"You were found about a hundred feet off the revetment, Rachel. I think you knew the wind was blowing that same direction, and you were trying to crawl away from it," Emma said, her tone sympathetic.

Closing her eyes, her hands on her face, Rachel kept seeing flashes of the incident. She felt terribly vulnerable, her emotions in tatters, and her hands fell away from her face. "I have these awful images…the smells, the sounds…"

"Post-Traumatic Stress Disorder," Emma said gently. Touching her hand, she whispered, "It's going to be with you for a while, Rachel. It's important not to fight it. In time, it will go away."

Gripping her cousin's hand, she said in a wobbly voice, "Thanks for being here."

"Hey, I'm glad I was."

"Was Khalid with you?"

"No, I was flying in alone to pick up another shipment of desks and books. He's up north with his sister Kinah. We're setting up a new village today. They're up there with the teacher and introducing her around to the village elders. I got a hold of them by GPS, satellite phone, and they know we're okay."

"Good," Rachel said, feeling stronger and more alert. Though, one thing puzzled her. "You said someone brought me here?"

Emma grimaced. "Hold on to your helmet. I was already here at the clinic helping to bring in the wounded when he arrived with you in his arms. I couldn't believe it." Emma gently held Rachel's scratched and bruised hand. "You'll never guess who brought you in.... Captain Tyler Hamilton. The dude who tried to get you flunked out of flight school back at Fort Rucker."

Chapter 2

"Where do you think you're going, Captain?"

Rachel was starting to slide off the gurney when a balding physician came over. His scowl deepened. "I feel fine, Doctor. I want to get out of here."

"Hold on, you've suffered smoke inhalation."

"I'm *fine*," Rachel insisted, remaining on the gurney. Emma had just left, and she wanted out of this crazy, busy place.

"No, you're not," the doctor said. "You've got first-degree burns in your throat from inhaling that smoke."

Coughing a little, Rachel said, "I figured that. But I want to get to my HQ. I want to make sure my copilot is all right." The fifty-something-year-old doctor rolled his eyes and then smiled.

"Captain, I've already sent an order to your CO to have you removed from the flight list for a week. You need time to let that throat of yours heal up."

"A *week* for a little smoke inhalation?" Rachel was more than a little stunned.

"Yes. Now, if you'll just sit still for about fifteen more minutes, I'll get one of my nurses over here to release you."

Shocked by the doctor's pronouncement, Rachel nodded. "I can do that, but I really don't want to not fly for seven days." That would leave her reflexes slower than usual. Rachel was used to flying every day or every other day. There were so many things to know about the Apache helicopter that it was imperative for pilots to fly often. This frequency kept them in rhythm with the multi-tasking demands made upon them.

The doctor shrugged. "Humor me, Captain. You're grounded for a week." He turned and left.

Rachel sat there gripping the sides of the gurney. Seven days was an eternity. And she felt helpless. She heard from others in the dispensary that three helicopters had been destroyed by the Taliban surprise attack. It had been a very bad day for Camp Bravo. Moving her legs back and forth out of boredom, Rachel watched the feverish pace of the dispensary. There were a lot of wounded men coming in. She was the only woman. How badly she wanted to get out of here and connect with Susan.

Her mind reverted back to what Emma had told her. How could Captain Tyler Hamilton be *here?* There were two transport squadrons at the CIA base. Apache pilots had nothing to do with them, unless used as escorts, because Chinooks lacked defenses and needed protection. Hamilton's voice was forever branded in her brain, and she would have recognized it in a heartbeat over the radio link. When did Hamilton arrive? God, she hoped his presence was temporary. Maybe he was with one of the Kandahar squadrons and had flown into the camp with some needed supplies. That meant he'd be gone by now. Back to wherever he came from. *Good riddance.*

Some relief flowed through Rachel. Her throat burned, and she reached over and picked up a glass of water sitting on a nearby stand. Of all the people in the world to rescue her! After setting the glass back on the stand, Rachel ran her fingers through her loose, dirty hair. Pieces of grass fell around her. She was filthy. All she wanted was to get the hell out of here, strip out of this smoky-smelling uniform and feel the cool water flowing across her. She could wash the dirt out of her hair, too.

A lot of old anger surfaced in her as she sat impatiently on the gurney. Hamilton had done his level best to scuttle her attempts to graduate out of Apache flight school. He was one of their top instructors. And she was the only woman in the all-male class. He'd had it in for her the moment he'd seen her at attention in the barracks. Rachel would never forget the surprise and then the raw anger that had leaped to his blue eyes as he spotted her. Her instincts told her that for some unknown reason, he'd hated her from Day One.

Rachel could never figure out why Hamilton hated her. Was it because she was a child of the Trayhern dynasty? Their family had given military service since this country had fought for its independence from England. The famous name had always preceded her. It was an honorable family tradition that most of the children of each generation would give at least six years of service to their country. Could Hamilton have hated her for that? Snorting, Rachel shook her head. Hamilton had been an enigma, always waiting for when she made a mistake to embarrass her in front of the other students. He said she couldn't fly like a man. And that is what got him in trouble.

The smell of alcohol and other antiseptics made Rachel wrinkle her nose. Couldn't she leave now? Every nurse was super busy with the wounded still coming in. Rachel pondered leaving on her own. And then she made the fatal error of looking up toward the entrance. Her lips parted in shock. Captain Tyler Hamilton walked right through the door. And he was looking for her.

Instantly, Rachel's heartbeat quickened and she gripped the gurney. Hamilton was six feet tall, lean and tightly muscled. He had military-short black hair, glacial-blue eyes, a strong chin and broad brow. He couldn't be looking for her? Impossible. How she wanted to disappear.

Anxiety and anger warred within her. Hamilton had tried to sink her career and smear her good family name. If it hadn't been for her uncle, Morgan Trayhern, Hamilton would have gotten away with it. The power that Morgan held in the military at every level had evened out the playing field. Her own father, Noah, had been in the Coast Guard for thirty years. He had flown into Fort Rucker to meet with the higher ups who had created the Apache flight program, along with her uncle Morgan. They met behind closed doors with the general. Hamilton had thought his power as an instructor pilot would bring her down and eject her from the program. He'd made a colossal mistake. No one tried to smear the Trayhern name like he had tried to do. In the end, Rachel had watched the general throw Hamilton out of the Apache program and send him to transport helicopters for the rest of his career. Further, he would never be promoted from captain. For the next twenty years he'd have no chance to climb in rank or to a better pay grade. Rachel had been told by her uncle Morgan about the behind-the-scenes change that had been made. She remembered clearly the shock written across Hamilton's face. He'd expected the general to kick her out of the program. Instead, he'd been the one jettisoned.

Lips tightening, Rachel sat back so that Hamilton couldn't see her. The bastard! She hated that he had rescued her. Five years had gone by and she'd never heard or seen him again. Until now. What kind of twisted irony was going on here? The man who hated her, who wanted her out of his training squadron had shown up again like the bad penny he was.

Rachel watched as he moved like a sinuous jungle cat through the busy dispensary. He found a nurse and talked to her. She gasped softly as the nurse turned and pointed directly at her cubicle. Damn! Hamilton turned and headed in her direction. Of all things, she didn't need this confrontation on top of all else!

Ty Hamilton approached the green-curtained cubicle where the nurse had sent him. He swallowed hard. The past was right in front of him as he walked around the desk, the other gurneys and the doctors dealing with the injured. Fear rose up in him as he drew closer to the cubicle. He couldn't see anyone, but the nurse had said Captain Trayhern was in there. He took a deep breath. With his right hand, he pulled back the curtain.

"Why the hell are you here?" Rachel snarled at him.

Taken aback, Hamilton stopped about three feet away from the gurney. The hardened look on Rachel's face made him go on the defensive. She was a beautiful woman even five years later. She'd matured and, if possible, in Ty's mind, was even lovelier than before. "I came to see if you were all right," he said in an even tone. That five years slammed back into him. She was angry. Rachel had always been a warrior. He'd seen it back in flight school. Now, sitting there, she looked like an eagle who was ready to defend over her kill. Only her gaze was directed at him.

"Get out of my life, Hamilton. I want *nothing* to do with you," she rasped.

Could he blame her for her rage? No. After all, he'd tried to deep-six her career. "Sorry, that's not going to happen."

"I don't care. Of all the people I never wanted to run into again, you're it."

He accepted her anger. In the five years since his removal by the general, who ran the Apache program, Ty had bitterly come to grips with his past. "Life is twisted, at best. You know that." He stood with his arms at his sides, his hands curving slightly. Captain Trayhern looked like she was going to leap off that gurney and attack him. His head spun with the violence of her reaction toward him. After all, he'd just saved her life. Was he expecting a thank-you? Apparently that wasn't going to happen. So why had he come looking for her? Ty didn't have an answer and that bothered him.

"No joke," Rachel snapped. She jabbed her finger in his direction. "Go back into whatever hole you crawled out of, Hamilton. I don't *ever* want to see you again. Do you understand me?"

His dark brows rose a little. Rachel's face became flushed, her gold-brown eyes narrowed on him like a hunter. He felt the full thrust of her hatred. After the secret decision by the general running the program to oust him due to his prejudice against women pilots, Ty had never seen her again. Not until now. "Five years is a long time to carry a grudge, isn't it?" he snarled back. "I just saved your friggin' life, in case you didn't realize it. If I hadn't seen you go down and the smoke covering you, you wouldn't be here right now."

Rachel squared her shoulders. "Well, let's just call it even then, shall we?"

Confused, he uttered, "What do you mean?"

"You tried to kill my career. I'll never forget what you tried to do to me. You lied to your superiors. You used every manipulation, every twist you could think of to get rid of me. I still don't know to this day why you targeted me, but that's water under the bridge. And if you saved my life, then I consider the slate between us clean. You tried to end my life back then. You saved it today."

Her raw, unfettered emotion made him step back. Apache pilots were, if nothing else, excellent killers. And the look on her face, the hoarse fury in her low voice was about killing—him. "So we're even?" he said.

"That's right, Hamilton. Now get out of my sight."

Stung, he saw Rachel point toward the opening between the curtains. Obviously, she was still reliving those events from the past. Wasn't it just like a woman to drag it into the present? In his experience, men let things like that go. They got on with life. He had. Until now. "Well, you aren't going to get your way," he warned her in a dark tone.

"What the hell are you talking about?" Anxiety sizzled through her. If Rachel had met him under any other circumstances, she'd have thought Hamilton damned handsome. Real eye candy. He appeared to be a cocky, arrogant flight jock when she'd first met him. His eyes were large and well spaced, his mouth full and certainly one that any woman would appreciate. His cheekbones were high and his black hair only accentuated his hard-jawed features.

Hamilton managed a twisted grimace with one corner of his mouth. Finally, the energy shifted to his side. "Our squadron was just assigned to Camp Bravo. We'll be stationed here for the next year." He saw the shock land across her pale features. A part of him, a tiny part, felt sorry for Rachel Trayhern. Her hair was in disarray, dirty and with bits of grass still buried in the strands. Her uniform was dusty, as well. When he'd seen her hit the asphalt and try to crawl away during the attack, he had no idea who she was. And when he'd run between the bullets and the lobbing grenades to reach her, Ty had only wanted to save a life.

Rachel felt his statement reverberate through her. She saw a bit of a savage gleam in his narrowing eyes. Realizing he was enjoying sharing that news with her made Rachel hate him even more. "You trash haulers aren't in our squadron area. That suits me fine." She'd deliberately called him a name she knew no transport helicopter pilot ever wanted to hear. The Apache pilots were the warriors of the Army helicopter fleet. Transport helos like the Chinook and their pilots were privately called "trash haulers" behind their backs. To hurl the words at him, however, was akin to throwing down the gauntlet between them once more. Rachel had no fear of this man. Her hatred of him trumped any thanks she might give him for saving her life today.

Hamilton stood there thinking through his options over her insult. The noise around them was a dull, constant roar. Doctors were yelling orders, orderlies were scrambling and nurses were hurrying at optimum speed as more injured were being brought in through the doors. Rachel was pale. She sat there coughing, her long, beautiful fingers pressed against her slender throat. Some of his anger over the insult dissolved. Without a word, he turned on his booted heel and left.

Rachel continued to cough. Relief sped through her as Hamilton exited. She watched him stalk angrily out of the dispensary, shoving the door open. It slammed against the building, he was that furious. Grabbing the glass, she poured water into it from a nearby container. She gulped the cooling liquid down her raw, burning throat and closed her eyes. She felt guilty. She shouldn't have, but she did. That bastard deserved every bit of hatred she had stored up within her. She opened her eyes and set the empty glass back on the stand.

"Captain, are you ready to leave?" A nurse with the name tag *Morayta, L.* came in. She had long, brown hair wrapped up in a knot behind her head, a stethoscope hanging around her neck. She had large, brown eyes that sparkled as she drew near.

"More than you could ever know," Rachel muttered. She had seen Lauren Morayta over at the chow hall from time to time. "You got my orders cut?"

Laughing, Lauren said, "I do." She scribbled her name on a piece of paper on her clipboard. "Dr. Henson wants to see you in three days. By then—" she turned to look around at the busy place "—we should be back to normal."

Taking the folded piece of paper, Rachel thanked her. "How many died in this attack?"

Lauren's smile disappeared. "Three so far. All burn casualties." She patted Rachel's hand. "You were the lucky one. The doctor wants you to rest for seven days."

Rachel didn't feel lucky. She slid off the gurney,

thanked the petite nurse and walked out of the chaotic dispensary. Outside, she gratefully breathed in the hot August air. Turning, Rachel walked back to her Black Jaguar Squadron headquarters. There was no way she was resting now. Black, oily smoke hung over the base like a funeral pall. Rachel could hear the roar of fire trucks over in the Ops area. She wondered if they needed help.

As she entered the busy tent, Rachel noticed how every office clerk was frantic and busy. Women were running here and there. It was an intense energy in the place as she stood just inside the door. To her relief, Rachel spotted her copilot, blond-haired Lieutenant Susan Cameron.

"Susan!" she called, hurrying over to her desk. "Are you okay?"

"Hey, Rachel. Yes, I am." She came around the desk and gave Rachel a hug of welcome. "Are you all right? I was in Ops when the attack came. I got the hell out of there and tried to find you. I never could. And then we got word from the clinic that you had suffered smoke inhalation but were going to be fine. I stayed here because they really needed me." Susan released her, relief in her gray eyes.

Rachel smiled. "It's going to take more than smoke to keep me down. Is anyone else from our squadron injured?"

"No. We're fine. Major Dallas Klein is going crazy, though."

"Why?"

"Because we've lost two Apaches."

"That sucks."

Shaking her head, Susan returned to her desk. "The major has her husband on the phone to the Pentagon right now. She's trying to find replacement Apaches for us. They aren't easy to find."

Rachel liked Major Mike Murdoch. He had joined the Army once again when his wife, Dallas, was given the BJS command in Afghanistan. "Well, if anyone can tear some Apaches loose, it's him." She rubbed her hands together. "I can hardly wait to get back in the saddle."

"Right now, we're two helos short," Susan murmured, worried. She sat down and pulled a pen from the pocket of her flight uniform. "I just hope the Pentagon doesn't screw us with wait time to get replacement Apaches. We keep our reflexes sharp because we're flying all the time."

Nodding, Rachel saw Major Klein emerge from her small office at the other end of the huge tent. She appeared grim. And when Dallas spotted her, some of that grimness fled from her expression for a moment. She seemed relieved to see her. The CO walked over.

"How are you, Rachel?" Dallas demanded.

"Fine, ma'am. Just some smoke inhalation. Nothing more."

"Good, good." Dallas looked around at the beehive of activity. "Helluva attack."

Rachel nodded. "Yes, ma'am, it was. The Taliban is really threatened by this base. It won't be the last time they try to move us out of their territory."

Dallas put her hands on her hips. She wore her usual one-piece green uniform. The BJS patch, a black jaguar snarling, was attached with Velcro on the left upper arm. The American flag was sewn on the left front of her uniform along with her last name. Embroidered yellow wings denoted she was an Apache pilot. "They screwed us royal, this time," she muttered, looking down at Susan and then over at Rachel. "They've never hit Apaches before."

"They got lucky," Susan said, lifting her head from her paperwork. "Before, they always lobbed grenades at the airstrip."

"Well," Rachel said, frowning, "they timed their attack better. We'd just landed and rolled to a stop in front of Ops. We use evasive tactics, change our flight path every day, but they got lucky this time."

"Unfortunately," Dallas agreed. "And I've got some bad news for you."

Rachel blinked. Her CO appeared grim. "Ma'am?" What on earth could this be about?

Susan looked up, surprise written on her face.

Dallas said in a low voice, "Major Murdoch just got off the phone with the Pentagon. He talked to Colonel Maya Stevens to see if we could get replacement Apaches for the two we just lost." Her thin brows fell. "We aren't getting replacements. All the new Apaches coming off Boeing's line are going directly to the Helmand Province in the south where all the action's at right now."

"But, ma'am, surely there are two somewhere," Rachel stammered, her mind spinning. If not, then she would be flying once a week. They were pilot rich right now, but with the loss of two birds, that would drastically change the pilot rotation.

"Tell me about it," Dallas griped. "What it comes down to is this—the four pilots who last flew those destroyed Apaches will be transferred out of BJS for six months. Instead, because all of you are CH-47 trained, you'll be sent to the new, incoming Chinook squadron that just arrived today. They're pilot poor and in need of more person power. They got the choppers but not enough qualified pilots. You four will fill in the ranks and help them out until we can get the two new Apaches in here."

"But..." Rachel choked out.

"But nothing," Dallas snapped. "You four are going to suck it up and do the dirty work."

"It wasn't our fault that our Apaches got targeted," Susan argued, distressed.

Of course, Dallas knew that no gunship pilot wanted to be relegated to a slow-moving, clunky transport helicopter. But it was clear she had no choice in the matter.

"You knew coming over here to our squadron that you could pull duty in the Chinooks. Now, you will." She turned to Rachel. "And you're on seven days' sick leave. That will give you plenty of time to refresh your knowledge of the Chinook and get up to speed."

Rachel felt as if the floor of the tent had fallen out from beneath her. Tyler Hamilton's squadron was the one she was speaking about. Her mouth went dry. "Ma'am, may I speak to you in private?"

Shrugging, Dallas said, "Of course. Follow me."

Once inside the small office, Dallas sat down behind her desk that was piled with work. Rachel stood at attention.

"At ease, Captain. What is it that you need to speak to me about in private?"

"Ma'am," Rachel choked out, placing her hands behind her back, "I can't be ordered over to that squadron." She launched into the details. Keeping it short, Rachel quickly explained her history.

Dallas seemed stricken by their information, but assumed a professional stance. "I can't help what happened to you in the past, Captain Trayhern. I have to run an all-woman squadron. We just lost two of our birds that we desperately needed. If you want to return to flying here when we get them, you have no other choice than to go over to that Chinook squadron."

"No question I want to remain here with BJS," Rachel said.

"What happened between you and Captain Hamilton was five years ago. Let dead dogs be buried." Dallas jabbed her finger toward Rachel. "And I don't want to hear that you're not getting along over there. You represent the United States, Captain. We're the only all-woman Apache squadron in the world, and I'll be damned if you're going to give us a black eye. Got it?"

Swallowing hard, Rachel whispered unsteadily, "Yes, ma'am. I got it."

"Dammit," Dallas growled, "make it work, Captain. I'm sorry that happened to you, but Hamilton got his just desserts. It's time to move on."

"I—I'm struggling with that," Rachel admitted hoarsely.

Dallas's eyes narrowed. "Captain, he just saved your life. That should count for something, shouldn't it? If he hadn't seen you go down and rescued you, we wouldn't be having this conversation, would we? Dismissed!"

Chapter 3

"Rachel?" Emma called as she popped into her tent in the BJS area, "I just heard what happened. Is it true?"

Rachel was at her small desk, squeezed into the corner of her tent. She turned in the chair and greeted her cousin. "Hey, I didn't expect to see you today."

"Got a minute?" Emma asked, sitting down on the end of her cot. "Is it true? Major Klein is moving the four of you over to the new transport squadron that just arrived? That she can't get her hands on two Apaches?"

Glumly, Rachel nodded and shut the manual on the Chinook she had been studying. "Yeah. Can you believe it?"

Emma reached out and touched her shoulder. "How are you? Your throat?"

"Better, thanks." Rachel gestured to the bottled water on her desk. "My throat has improved a lot since yesterday's attack. The doc ordered me to stand down for seven days because of smoke inhalation, but I'm fine."

Emma set her helmet bag on the wooden floor. "Is there anything Khalid and I can do for you?"

"Aside from Khalid buying me an Apache helo to strap my butt into, no," Rachel chuckled.

Emma nodded with a smile. "I remember when I was flying Apaches and then was ordered to fly the Chinook. I hated the slow-moving transport. Besides that, you're wide open for attack. All I had was a tail gunner at the rear of the helo. I felt like a piece of raw meat hung out in the sky with a sign that said 'shoot me.'"

"I know." Rachel liked the fact that now Emma was allowed to wear civilian clothes instead of a uniform. Her hair was growing longer and it suited her. Today she had on a dark green, one-piece flight suit with her name on it. "How are things in your neck of the woods? I was over at communications at HQ, and it seems pretty quiet out there today."

"It is," Emma agreed. "Usually, when the Taliban makes a big attack, they run and hide for a week. They don't want Apache wrath out hunting for them."

"Major Klein is like a madwoman on a wolf hunt over there," Rachel agreed. "She wants to find and blow them out of existence." And then sadly, "I wish I was in one of those Apaches. This is hell, Emma. I know I went and learned how to fly a Chinook transport, but that was years ago." She held up her hands. "This is like starting all over."

"Hmm," she agreed, "it is." Her brows drew down. "And is it true you're going into Hamilton's Chinook squadron?"

Rachel groaned. "Yes. The old squadron did its tour

of duty, and now Hamilton had been ordered in to replace it. And you know the worst of it? He's the CO!"

Emma shook her head. "I didn't know that."

"Ever since Hamilton was removed from the Apache program, he's been in CH-47s. That's five years. Plenty of time to become a CO of a squadron."

"I guess he kept his nose clean since then," Emma said with a twisted smile.

"He's a captain. He'll never rise higher in rank than that, no matter how long he stays in the Army and flies those transports," Rachel growled.

"And you're studying the CH-47 manual to bone up? When do you have to go over there?"

"Read this," Rachel told her cousin, and handed her the order she'd just received.

"Oh, God," Emma whispered, frowning. "Not only is Hamilton CO, but he's the IP? Instructor pilot?"

"It's like the universe has it in for me. Not only do I get to live with this bastard for the next six months, he has to qualify me in the CH-47. How's that for double jeopardy? I've been racking my brain trying to figure a way out of this."

"Can you get out of it?"

With a shake of her head, Rachel sighed. "Major Klein made it clear that if I want to fly the Apache when it arrives in six months, I have to sit my butt in that CH-47 and do the duty. If I refuse to fly a transport, then I'll be shipped out to another Apache squadron. You know how important it is that women fly together. You've done it. There's a camaraderie between us that no male squadron will ever have. I love it here, Emma. I don't want to give that up."

Gripping her cousin's slumped shoulder, Emma said soothingly, "Hey, I understand. I loved flying with the

Black Jaguar Squadron in Peru and then here. We're making history. We're showing everyone that a group of women can do as well as any male squadron or mixed squadron."

"That's the other problem," Rachel warned her. "Hamilton's squadron is all men. Then all of a sudden, he's getting four female Apache drivers thrown into the mix. Because he hates women and loves spreading his crap that we're not cut out for flying or war, this is going to be a nightmare for all of us."

"How are the other gals taking the assignment?"

"Better than I am. But they don't have the past history with Hamilton like I do. They were in other training outfits, not mine."

"This sucks, dude," Emma agreed, placing her hands in her lap. "Could you use some interesting news that Khalid got wind of the other day?"

Rachel perked up. "Sure. What has he heard?"

Emma leaned forward. "You have to keep this top secret."

"Oh, I will," Rachel promised, seeing the glint in her cousin's eyes. "Whatever it is, it's big!"

Laughing a little, Emma said, "Oh, it's an eye-knocker-outer."

"What? Tell me!"

Emma grinned. "There's a new Black Jaguar group forming under Colonel Maya Stevens. Khalid has been working with Maya and her husband, Dane, who were both assigned to the Pentagon. Maya was the creator of the original BJS, and she showed the boys in the Army how to use the Apache to stop the drug runners in Peru."

"Oh, she's famous for that. She's the bedrock of the

BJS," Rachel enthused, excited. "But what is this new BJS squadron?"

"Not a flight squadron." Emma's eyes glinted. "It's a U.S. Marine initiative. They've asked her and Dane to head up a group of women volunteers from the five military services who will have boots on the ground. They're specialists in language and Afghan culture. Their job is to be put in individual Marine deployment squadrons that are coming here."

Confused, Rachel said, "Women in combat?"

"Yes, with a particular mission. They're in training with the Marines right now at Camp Pendleton. Come October, they're going to arrive here, at Bravo Camp. This will be their HQ. Maya will head it up because she knows how to integrate women into all male elements. It's not flying but Maya will also be working with transport squadrons here, as well as Apache deployment."

Rachel gasped at the information. "My God, it's really happening. These women are being trained for combat roles among the Marine squadrons?"

"Yes. There will be one woman per assigned Marine squad out in the country working with villages and elders. There's a whole new effort to win hearts and minds here. And Maya was arguing this right up to the halls of Congress. She told the senators in a closed-door session that if they used women who spoke the language and worked with the wives of the elders in a given village, that more loyalty, more contact and far more information would be shared." Emma grinned. "You know how women talk to one another. These women are being trained as paramedics, too. They'll be able to give vaccinations, treat the children, wives and female elders of the village."

"What a brilliant idea!" Rachel said, amazed and excited. "Brilliant!"

"Khalid has been friends with Maya and Dane for years, so he got the inside scoop. Don't breathe a word of this. The fun part is that you will be interfacing with BJS ground troops because you'll be flying the Marine squads out with these women. Maya felt that having an all-woman BJS squadron here already would help give these ground-troop women the support they need."

"Is the Marine Corps happy about this?" Rachel wondered.

"For the most part, yes. But you know the Marines— only a man can fight. There's a lot of resentment among some of them, but Dane is working with the sergeants who command these squadrons. There's no room for prejudice out on the ground. All you care about is that the person next to you, regardless of whether they are male or female, can shoot and kill."

"And these women are volunteers?"

"Yes, all five services are represented, even the Coast Guard."

"And they're enlisted?"

"Yes. Maya and Dane chose from among all the volunteers. These are women with at least four years in the military. They are the cream of the crop. This idea was put into overdrive almost a year ago. These women had to learn an Afghan language, complete paramedic training and then go to Camp Pendleton in California to become rifle qualified. They're the whole package."

"That is incredible," Rachel whispered. She saw the happiness glowing in Emma's face. "Leave it to Maya to break down more doors. While the squad leader is dealing with the male elders, the woman soldier can be talking to the elder's wife. I'll lay you ten to one she'll get more info from that wife than the sergeant or lieutenant ever will from the man."

Nodding, Emma said with a grin, "That's exactly what Maya is counting on."

"Wow," Rachel murmured. "Does Major Klein know about this? She must. She was Maya's executive officer down in Peru."

"Oh, she sure does. Dallas is excited about it, too. She's gung ho on the whole BJS ground program."

"They'll be together again like they were in Peru. That's kismet, because we both know they were a successful team down there in stopping drug cartels from getting cocaine out of Peru. The Pentagon, the Chief of Staff know that when Maya and Dallas were a pair, things got done right."

"And their past history and record probably enabled this program to go forward."

"Absolutely," Emma said. She rubbed her hands together and added, "Kick butt, take names."

Laughing, Rachel felt some of her depression lift. Emma was always the positive one. No matter what life had thrown at her, she made mud pies out of the mud. She never let something bad, like the loss of sensation in two fingers of her left hand, stop her. The Army might have discharged her for that, but being married to Khalid had brought her right back here. Reaching out, Rachel gripped Emma's hand for a moment, "I'm so glad you're here."

"Listen, you need to get square with Hamilton." Emma released her hand, her voice lowered with concern. "When do you have to see him?"

"Today." She looked down at her watch on her right wrist. "Matter of fact, at 1400 I have to officially get inducted into his CH-47 squadron."

"Ugh. Not only is he your CO, he's your flight instructor."

"How lucky can a girl get, right?"

Emma shook her head. "Well, we know that life is never fair, but this sucks. Will you be okay, Rachel?"

"I don't know," she said, looking around the tent that had been her life with BJS. "I have such anger toward him. It just bubbles up and it surprises even me. I didn't know how much I hated him until he showed up at the dispensary yesterday. Everything, and I mean everything, came back from my flight school days. I was so surprised at how cold and angry I was."

"How are you going to deal with it? Because the Army doesn't much like it when personal stuff gets in the way of your duties."

"I'll conduct myself as an officer and work to be neutral toward him."

"You can't afford to flunk out on flying the CH-47."

"Oh, don't worry, I won't. I'm keeping my eye on the prize—in six months, I'll be rotated back to BJS and I'll strap an Apache on my ass again." Rachel gave her a twisted grin. "I have my priorities straight, believe me. I might hate him, but I'll be all business in the cockpit."

"That's going to be so hard," Emma said.

Rachel shrugged. "I'm thirty years old. I've been around the block. I guess it's my time to suck it up, see it for what it is—a test."

Emma chuckled. "Spoken like a true Trayhern."

Rachel nodded and smiled. "My parents have emailed me about it. They always have good advice about stuff like this. My dad said to just keep my eye on the future and try the best I can to remain detached about Hamilton."

Emma giggled. "I know your mom. She's a take-no-prisoners woman. What did she say?"

"Because she was one of the first women police detectives down at Miami-Dade, she said to not take anything personally. That I needed to be responsible for every action, every word I had to speak to Hamilton. And to keep a daily journal of what happened so that, in case this all goes to hell in a handbag, I have notes to rely on, not my memory."

Emma laughed fully. "Aunt Kit is a realist. I like her approach. Uncle Noah is always so philosophical about life. And she's brass tacks all the way."

"I think I got the best from both of them. I really want my position back with BJS. I'll go through this hazing with Hamilton and gut it out. But I'll also be chronicling my time with him. He sideswiped my career once. I won't let him do it again."

Emma looked toward the tent flap opening and then lowered her voice. "I had Khalid do a little inquiry into Hamilton's career since he got kicked out of Fort Rucker. He's been a good boy according to the records. But what is against him is that he's been in all-male helo squadrons since then. He's never had to interface with female pilots again. And Khalid is worried that, by you being ordered over there, this could upset his apple cart. You know that the general told Hamilton that if he ever showed one prejudicial moment against another woman, he was kicking him out of the Army." Emma straightened and she pointed toward the tent flaps. "Khalid thinks Hamilton won't try to sabotage you like he did before."

"I hope you're right," Rachel whispered fervently. "Thank Khalid for getting the dirt on Hamilton. I appreciate it."

"Well," Emma said, "if the truth be known, Uncle Morgan was already looking into it. You know he has contacts right up to the president. Khalid bumped into him at the Pentagon. When they discovered they were trying to find out more about Hamilton, they joined forces."

"The Trayherns stick together!" Rachel laughed. "It makes me feel good Uncle Morgan is in there pitching for me."

"You know he won't allow anyone to harm us in any way," Emma said. She lowered her voice. "As a matter of fact, Khalid found out something that just shocked me."

"What?"

"Your father called Uncle Morgan and told him what was going on with Hamilton trying to get you dropped out of the flight program. What no one can know is that Uncle Morgan had a direct pipeline into the general running the program. And Morgan asked the general to release Hamilton. And he did."

Rachel sighed. "I was told about it shortly after Hamilton was out of the program. I didn't realize you didn't know."

Emma smiled tightly. "No one messes with the Trayhern children. Uncle Morgan will see to that." She reached out. "So, just be aware that Uncle Morgan will be watching the reports being sent to the Pentagon by Hamilton. He'll be monitoring him like a hawk." Patting her arm, Emma said, "You have a guardian angel at your back, Cousin. You just haul your share of this load and do it right. The moment Hamilton steps out of line, Uncle Morgan is going to quietly insert himself into the equation and make damn sure he's booted out of the Army for good."

Pleasure and reassurance thrummed through Rachel. "Thank you for the pep talk. I really appreciate it. It makes going over there less nerve-racking for me."

"Well, you have to carry yourself with integrity at all times," Emma warned. "You can't lower your guard and get angry or throw a temper tantrum around him. You have to be bulletproof, Cousin. Be the officer that you are. You're a Trayhern and you have honor. If he tries anything, Hamilton will be in a world of hurt. Uncle Morgan needs you to keep your record clean."

"Got it," Rachel said. "This is incredible. My dad filled me with stories of the military and all the Trayherns that have served over the last two hundred plus years...but I never realized until this happened how powerful they really are in the military world."

"Thank Uncle Morgan. He's the head honcho. And like I said, he's got the ear of every military general in the U.S.A." She grinned and stood up. "That plus the president."

Standing up, she hugged Emma. "Thank you, Cousin."

Emma leaned down to pick up her helmet bag. "I hope Hamilton realizes by now he can't screw around with a Trayhern."

Opening the flap to her tent, Rachel said, "We're going to find out in a couple of hours."

Emma slipped through the flaps and lifted her hand. "I'll be in touch...."

Turning, Rachel allowed the flaps to fall together. The August heat made the tent stuffy. She wiped her brow and sat back down to continue reading the CH-47 flight manual. A lot of her stomach churning had settled with Emma's good news. She had even more reason to make this unholy alliance work. But would Hamilton plan on making her look bad again? Or had he really learned his lesson?

Chapter 4

Ty Hamilton dragged in a deep breath. The next woman he had to see was the one he didn't want to ever see again. His clerk had just told him that Captain Rachel Trayhern had arrived. He hit the button on the intercom.

"Tell her to come in," he ordered.

"Yes, sir."

Stomach in knots, Ty wondered if she was still pissed off at him for saving her life a week ago. Sitting behind his desk, he saw the door open. Rachel Trayhern looked a lot different today. Her brown hair was caught up in a knot at the nape of her slender neck. Her dark green flight uniform was clean instead of dirty. She wore no makeup, but she didn't have to, he thought. Willing himself to ignore her natural beauty, he watched her as she turned and shut the door. Then she came and stood at attention in front of his desk, her face unreadable. But her cheeks were red and Ty knew she was upset. Back in flight school, when Rachel was angry, her cheeks were like two red spots on her flawless face.

"Captain Trayhern reporting as ordered," she said, tight-lipped.

"At ease, Captain," Ty said. He gestured to a chair that sat near his desk, on her left. "Have a seat. We have a lot to discuss."

"Yes, sir." Rachel tried to ferret out how Hamilton really felt about meeting her again. This time, it was on equal footing rank-wise. She wasn't a newbie to flight school. Heart pounding, she kept a grip on her clipboard and sat down.

Ty flipped through a sheaf of papers and located her personnel record. As he opened it, he glanced in her direction. She sat at attention in the straight-backed chair. His heart squeezed over the hardness in her golden eyes. There wasn't a trace of an emotion on her oval face. Her lips were compressed. Okay, he deserved that reaction. Five years hadn't healed the wound. He got it.

"Your record indicates that you took CH-47 flight school training four years ago."

"Yes, sir, I did."

Nodding, Ty kept his voice neutral. "And you have forty hours in them?"

"Yes, sir."

"Well, it's obvious you need retraining, and I've set up flights with my scheduling sergeant. You will assume copilot duties from now on. We'll be flying every day." He held her hard gaze. "I'm the instructor pilot in our squadron. But you probably knew that."

"I make it a point to know," Rachel said in a low, tight tone. She searched his face. It would be easy to continue to hate him if he weren't so drop-dead good-looking. Eye candy for sure, Rachel thought. Tyler Hamilton was the perfect poster boy for an internet ad by the U.S. Army to lure young men who wanted adventure.

"Of course," he murmured, looking down at her file. He reached to his right, picked up the squadron patch and dropped it on the edge of the desk nearest to her. "You'll be wearing the Raven Squadron patch from now on. At least for the six months that you're assigned to us."

Rachel desperately wanted to keep her BJS patch on the left sleeve of her uniform. But she knew she had to relinquish it. Distastefully, she picked up the other patch. It burned in her fingers. She wanted to angrily throw it on the floor but didn't. The flicker in his eagle-like gaze revealed how carefully he watched her for any reaction. Did Hamilton still have it in for her? Rachel assumed he did. Every day in the cockpit with this bastard would be like being sent to the dungeon for torture.

"Do you have any questions?" he demanded, feeling as if he were addressing a wooden doll, beautiful but completely detached from him. Ty could have wished for a warmer response.

The other three women from BJS whom he'd also be training, had been open, smiling and enthused to be here to fly. But not Rachel. A sense of defeat flowed through him. He had hoped five years had buried the hatchet between them. Casting around for a topic, he asked, "Have you been cleared by the physician on your smoke inhalation?"

"Yes, sir, I have." She took a paper from her clipboard and dropped it on his desk. "I've been cleared to fly and ordered back to duty."

"Excellent," he said. "I'll speak to my sergeant about putting you on the flight schedule for tomorrow. In the meantime, go out to the Ops desk and get your paperwork filled out. Sergeant Johnson will give you the scoop on what you need as a copilot in our squadron. Welcome."

He rose and extended his hand to her. Stiffly, Rachel got to her feet but refused to shake his hand. "With all due respect, Captain Hamilton, I have to be here for six months, and that's it. May I be dismissed?"

The iciness in her tone shocked him. It was war, not peace between them. He withdrew his hand. "Dismissed."

The door opened and shut. Ty moved from behind his desk. The squadron had arrived just yesterday to replace the other one, which was being rotated home to the United States. He'd been here at Camp Bravo for two weeks with his transport pilots, learning the lay of the land and picking up information from the outgoing pilots. Right now, his squadron was ready to go in one of the most dangerous places in Afghanistan to fly.

Walking around the desk, hands on his hips, Ty smarted from Rachel Trayhern's demeanor. She'd refused to shake his hand. Why had he expected the white flag between them? She probably thought he was going to try and tarnish her record. Stopping, Ty raised his head, his lips pursed. She was all business. No anger in her eyes. No fear. Just that cold hardness. A real ice queen. But then he remembered back in flight school, at the beginning, how warm and open she'd been. The more he rode her during the instruction flights, the less warm and open Rachel became. He wondered if the warmth had returned in any capacity. Was she like this with everyone? Or just him?

Sighing, Ty knew he had no one but himself to blame. But dammit, he'd paid the ultimate price for his stupidity, too. In the last five years, he'd tried to reestablish his good name. And to a degree, he had. When the colonel made him squadron commander last year, Ty had drawn a sigh of relief. He thought for sure that they'd never give him a command. Now, a year into it, he'd led well. But then, there were no women pilots in his squadron, either. Now, he had four of them for six months. Damn. What a test.

From the very beginning he fought liking Rachel Trayhern. He'd found her amazingly beautiful in flight school. Everyone had responded to her like welcoming sunlight. Back then, he'd been jealous, angry. She not only was poised and confident but carried the vaunted Trayhern name. Hamilton was well aware that the Trayherns had served with honor in all of the military branches for hundreds of years. They truly were a military family dynasty. And he'd been jealous of that, too.

Running his fingers through his short, black hair, Ty circled around his desk and sat down. He had a lot of planning to do with four new pilots suddenly on board. Oh, no question he could use them. His other male pilots wouldn't have a problem with them. They didn't carry the belief that women were weak and would always be less than a man, like he had in the past.

Rachel took in a deep breath of air as she left the Ops area of the control tower. In her arms, she had more information about Raven Transport Squadron than she cared to have. The sunlight was welcome, the August morning heating up. There was plenty of activity on the tarmac. The second Apache rolled down the recently patched runway for takeoff. The first was already in the air, heavily loaded with armament. How she wished she could be there and not here!

Sadness moved through her as she walked between the tent cities that were set up on the covert base. Bravo sat on top of an eight-thousand-foot mountain. It was the nearest CIA base to the Afghanistan-Pakistan border, always a juicy target for the Taliban. The two Apaches that had been targeted and burned had been bulldozed off the runway. They sat like mangled, broken birds on the other side, and it hurt Rachel to look at them.

"Get your head screwed on straight, Trayhern," she muttered to herself as she turned down a dirt avenue to her tent. Pushing the flaps aside, she dropped all the gear, manuals and papers onto her cot.

"Hey," Emma called, opening one of the flaps, "how did it go?"

Turning, Rachel smiled a hello over to her cousin. "Flying in or out this morning?"

"Out," Emma said, tucking her flight gloves in the side pocket of her uniform. "How'd it go with Hamilton? You look pale."

Sitting down after offering Emma her other chair, Rachel said grumpily, "It went. I was so angry at him."

"And him?"

Shrugging, Rachel muttered, "He did all the right things, Emma. I couldn't see or detect that he still had it in for me."

"Did he look happy to see you?" She grinned.

"I don't know. Honestly, he had a poker face, too."

"And so did you."

"Guilty," she admitted, frowning. "It was just weird. When he tossed the squadron patch on his desk, I had this infantile reaction to grab it, throw it on the floor and stomp on it." She laughed.

"Hey, you have a right to feel like that." Emma smiled. "But like the good officer you are, you didn't allow your personal feelings to make it a messy situation."

"It was hard," she admitted, rubbing her hands down the thighs of her flight suit. "I kept trying to ferret out his hate for me. Or his anger. All I saw was officer decorum."

"Well, that might be good news then." Emma raised her brows. "Maybe he's learned his lesson, that female pilots are just as good as male pilots?"

Rachel shrugged. "I'll find out, won't I?"

"Oh, I don't think he's going to do anything but treat you right, Cousin. After all, he has everything to lose if he doesn't."

"I thought of that angle, too," Rachel said. "I can barely tolerate that he's going to be my flight instructor—again." Lifting her eyes to the tent ceiling, she said, "I wonder what I did to deserve this a second time, Emma. Talk about double jeopardy."

"Take it one day at a time," Emma counseled. She stood up and patted Rachel on her slumped shoulder. "Do the things we talked about earlier. I'm off to take a load of books, children's clothes and shoes to a village north of here."

"Be careful...."

"Oh, always!" Emma leaned over and gave Rachel a quick hug. "See you on the return. I'm due back at sunset. Maybe we can have a cup of coffee over at the chow hall then?"

"I'd like that," Rachel said. Even though Emma was now a civilian, she had access to the chow hall to eat, just like anyone in the military would. Watching her cousin leave, she felt buoyed by her presence. Emma was always positive. But then, Emma had not encountered a female-hating flight instructor, either.

Rising, she walked over to the cot. The squadron patch showed a black raven in flight. Rachel resisted putting it on and placed it on the table. She'd do it tomorrow morning. Until then, she still wanted to wear her BJS patch, a source of pride and honor to her. There was a lot to do. She had to go to BJS Ops and turn in her helmet gear. The ugly-looking transport helmet would have to be worn instead. It was all so distasteful, like she was being thrown back into hell again....

The morning air was cold at eight thousand feet. Out on the flight line, everyone's breath created white clouds when they spoke. Bundled in her flight jacket and gloves, Rachel moved slowly around the Chinook helicopter. It was the workhorse of Afghanistan. Carrying men, supplies, ammo, food and aviation fuel, the bird could do it all. She listened to Ty Hamilton as they performed the mandatory walkaround duties. Having studied the manuals, Rachel had already memorized the things she needed to check on the helicopter before ever entering the cockpit.

The sun was still below the horizon, the stars visible high in the dark sky. The crew was busy getting this helo prepped for takeoff. Today, Hamilton was flying boxes of ammunition, MREs, meals ready to eat, to an Army outpost in a valley north of the camp. As he went over their schedule for the day, Rachel tried not to like Hamilton's low voice. He was thorough and instructive but not arrogant as he had been in flight school. That was good, because Rachel would not tolerate that attitude from him now.

At the open ramp at the end of the helo, a load master, responsible for getting supplies into the huge bay, was busy. The other young, red-haired man was their gunner.

"The only protection we have is our gunner," Ty told her as they stood near the yawning ramp, which lay against the surface of the tarmac. "Once we're ready to lift off, he'll put the machine gun up in the center, there—" and he pointed to a square cut out of the platform surface "—and settle it into it and lock it. Then he'll be sitting down, legs between it, hands on the weapon. We keep the ramp down while we fly. He's our eyes and ears back here, and we'll be relying heavily on anything he sees. We'll take the ramp up shortly before we do any landing."

Nodding, Rachel knew there was little evasive protection in the Chinooks. Unlike the Apache, which could instantly know when a SAM missile or a grenade launcher was fired, this workhorse had no such protection. "It falls on the eyes and ears of the crew," she agreed. Rachel made sure she didn't have to stand any closer to Hamilton than necessary. They both wore dark green baseball caps on their heads and Nomex fire retardant gloves. It was below freezing and the Nomex warmed their hands.

"Yes," Ty murmured. "At this outpost, there's a landing area so we can set down, and our crew can get the supplies off-loaded with the help of the squad."

"Good to hear." Rachel understood that these outposts often sat on peaks high above the valley so the Army squad manning them could use their binoculars or rifle scopes to keep watch on the Afghans who farmed the valleys below. These squadrons stayed for three months and got to know the farmers. In knowing them, they could spot outsiders who were Taliban, sneaking through the area to attack American soldiers. And then they could be captured or killed.

"Let's saddle up," Hamilton told her, walking up the ramp and into the helo.

Following him, Rachel nodded to the two enlisted men in the rear. She saw no reason to be cold and standoffish with them. They had already secured the cargo with netting. She eased between the nylon seats on the side of the helo and the load. Hamilton climbed up the stairs and took the right seat, the pilot's position.

Her mind and focus were on her flying. Easing into the left-hand seat, Rachel picked up her new helmet and settled it on her head. Relieved that Hamilton was already busy, she got out her preflight cheat sheet and strapped it on her thigh. There was always a list of things to do before taking off. This was standard on any aircraft or helicopter. Plugging in the jack to the radio intercom, Rachel pulled the mike close to her lips. Hamilton had done the same.

Within ten minutes, they'd completed their preflight check. Once they had harnessed up, Rachel wondered if he would allow her to take off.

"I'll do the lifting," Hamilton told her as if reading her mind. "And once we're in the air, I'll hand the controls over to you."

"Okay," Rachel said. They were going to a dangerous area. Taliban were known to hide in the scrub brush that peppered the outpost area and wait for the helo. Other Chinooks had been fired upon earlier, so this was no familiarization flight. Already, Rachel could feel the adrenaline pouring into her bloodstream. The moment they lifted off, they were targets. She felt horribly naked without an Apache strapped to her butt.

She continued to find out what her copilot duties were as Hamilton fired up the first engine and then the second one. There was a sense of familiarity with the helo, and it made her relax to a degree. In no time, the crew was ready for takeoff.

Ty had pulled down the dark shield from his helmet in order to protect his eyes from the rising sun's rays. He noticed that Rachel had done the same. That didn't stop him from being aware that her profile was clean, her nose straight and her lips full. She was beautiful, even if half her face was hidden. Trying to ignore his male reaction to her, he said, "We're at the top end of weight limits with this cargo. And in the predawn hours, there's more humidity in the air than when the sun is up. That means it's harder for this helo to lift off. So, on days like this, I start her up by taxiing her the length of the airport runway. That way, by the time I hit the end of it, I'm applying full power, and it's easier for the bird to lift off."

"Plus," Rachel said, "it saves us fuel." She was always taxiing the Apache the same way. It saved fuel. And when they were in a hot spot, they needed to keep all the fuel so that they could protect the soldiers and Marines on the ground.

"Roger that," Hamilton agreed. "Okay, here we go."

Rachel focused entirely on the takeoff. One of the main attributes of an Apache pilot was laser-like focus and ability to multitask. Although she sat there, hands resting on her thighs, she watched the instruments, watched Hamilton's hands and absorbed it all. The Chinook groaned, and the blades thunked and whirled faster and faster. Finally, they were taxiing.

The Chinook was laborious as it trundled down the airstrip like a weighted elephant, the blades whipping at maximum. The helo shook and trembled. As they moved down the strip Rachel wondered if Hamilton would even reach takeoff speed, but he did. The end of the runway came up, and the bird lifted easily into the dawn sky. Rachel didn't want to tell Hamilton that he had done a good job. She wasn't ready to give him a compliment.

"Okay, you have the controls," he told her.

Quickly sliding her hands around the stick and collective, she repeated back to Hamilton. "I've got the controls."

"Releasing controls," he affirmed and lifted his hands away. Ty had expected the Chinook to suddenly fall a few feet, but it didn't. Rachel took over and the bird was climbing. There was no sign that one pilot had stopped flying and another had taken over. She was good. But then, he bitterly reminded himself, she was an Apache pilot. They were the cream of helicopter aviation. Deep in his heart, he was still bitter over what had happened, but he had no one to blame but himself.

"Nice job," he complimented her.

Rachel was stunned that he'd said anything. Her gloves tightened momentarily around the stick and collective. Her mouth quirked, though she kept quiet. She damn well knew how to fly a helo, even if it was this bulky, noisy bird that crawled through the sky.

Hamilton frowned. He'd expected some kind of response from her, but that icy profile was all he saw. He forced himself to stop expectations, and just continued to look out the cockpit windows for any sign of a SAM missile. They were climbing five thousand feet to avoid the grenade launchers, but a missile could blow them out of the sky at any time. Rubbing his chin, he tried not to feel hurt by Trayhern's cold composure. She had smooth flight hands. Although the CH-47 shook around them, the roar always present, it rode the air currents without a bobble or jerk.

As he sat there in his seat, Ty tried to protect himself and remain immune to Rachel. He saw no ring on her finger, although to be fair about it, pilots never wore such things. If they ever crashed and were found by the Taliban, there had to be no identification on them. Except for their name, rank and serial number. Still, he wondered if she was married. And to whom?

Chapter 5

Rachel loved flying, even if it was a slow transport helo. The shaking and shuddering of the twin blades located at each end of the long, tubular helicopter soothed. It helped her relax instead of becoming tense in the cockpit with Hamilton. The day was beautiful. The sharp, brown peaks of the mountains had little foliage on them except for stubborn brush. They looked like green dots on the slopes.

"Okay, fly around that mountain and you're going to see a village. We're going to land there first. Then we'll take off and fly up to the outpost situated two thousand feet above it."

Frowning, Rachel said, "That wasn't in the orders. We're to fly the cargo to the outpost."

Ty saw her lips set in a stubborn line. "We don't put in the landing at the village because it's automatically assumed by scheduling," he explained. "There's a Special Forces team that moves up and down this narrow valley. We have some antibiotics and other medicine to drop off to their paramedic on the team."

Nodding, Rachel knew that the Chinooks were the only supply line to the Special Forces men. She had high regard for them.

"Plus," Ty said, a bit of humor in his tone, "their captain ordered up a bunch of bags of candy. It's for the kids. They love it."

She cut him a glance. He was smiling, and she'd never seen that before. Ever! Forcing herself to focus back on her flying, she felt angry. Why? Not having time to examine the feeling, she took the helo around the tall, barren peak. Up ahead, she could see a small village and an area that had been scraped free of rocks for helo landing.

Pointing, Ty told her, "Head for that flat place outside the village. We always land there."

"What about the threat of Taliban?" she demanded. Rachel always got spooked when they were near the mountains. Taliban hid in the caves and behind the huge boulders to keep from being seen. All it would take is one grenade launcher fired from the slope down on that meager landing zone to blow up the Chinook.

"Always a possibility." Ty took binoculars and began to focus on the slopes above the village. "Normally, we get an Apache escort, but with two destroyed, we go it alone."

Rachel's mouth tightened. She felt the fear leaking through her bloodstream. Her heart picked up in beat. She knew how important the Apaches were to the transport squadron. They had infrared, a television camera, and they would make routine sweeps of the area to find and locate hidden Taliban. Then they would take them out with rocket or Gatling gun fire, making it safe for the unarmed Chinook to land or drop off cargo to the outposts. "Don't remind me," she gritted out.

Surprised at the anger he heard in her low tone, Ty didn't respond. Rachel wasn't happy about being here. It was obvious she wanted no part of any of this. Scanning the slopes, he said, "So far, so good. I don't see enemy."

Snorting softly, Rachel knew that no matter how good Hamilton was at trying to spot Taliban, they could fool him by hunkering down and being invisible as they flew by the area. "You won't see them until it's too late," she said.

As they rounded the slope of the mountain, Ty put the binoculars away. He called for the gunner to remove the machine gun. Then he brought up the ramp and closed it on the Chinook. "This is the way it is," he told her. Pointing, he said, "Land it now."

Rachel did as she was ordered. It had been a long time since she'd landed this bulky helicopter. Unlike the streamlined Apache, this workhorse was like a teetering elephant on a small three-legged stool. As she slowly brought the helo down, the blades kicked up fierce clouds of yellow dust. It quickly turned into a situation that all pilots hated. They had to land blind. She couldn't see anything and she couldn't see the ground. A ribbon of panic ate through her.

"It's okay," Hamilton soothed. "You're doing fine. Just keep going down at the same rate. You'll feel the wheels touch in a second."

Sweat popped out on Rachel's lip. Hamilton's reassuring voice was exactly what she needed. Trusting his analysis of the blinding situation, she suddenly felt the tires anchor to the ground. Relief shot through her. Instantly, Hamilton's hands were flying over the instruments, and he shut down the helicopter's two huge whirling blades.

Sagging back into the chair, Rachel let out a sigh of relief. She began to unharness.

"I'm staying with the bird," Hamilton told her. "I want you to go in the back. Once the load master gets the boxes out from the netting, walk with him to the village. My sergeant will meet with the Spec Forces team and hand off the supplies. Then go with that captain. You need to get to know the elders. We always take these boxes of food and candy every time we fly in." He turned and grinned a little. "It's called nation building."

Nodding, Rachel pulled off her helmet. She tried to remain immune to his very male smile. He'd pushed the dark visor up off his face. His blue eyes were wide and she saw happiness in them. Hamilton obviously enjoyed doing this. She didn't. "I feel like a naked chicken on a NASCAR raceway," she growled as she got up. Making sure she didn't brush against the other pilot, Rachel added, "We're a really big target right now."

Nodding, Hamilton said, "Get used to it. We don't get Apache escort as often as we'd like. Besides, this village, just FYI, is pro-America. They know when we come, and they send people up on the slopes to make sure no Taliban are lurking around. If they did find them, they'd have come down to tell the captain. And then he'd put a call in to us because he knows the flight and our call sign. So, it's as safe as it can be."

That was good news to Rachel. She saw Hamilton pull the lever that would lower the huge ramp at the other end of the Chinook. One pilot always remained with a bird on the ground. In case of unexpected attack, the engines could be revved up, the other pilot and people could jump on board, and they would take off. "Okay, thanks for the info," she said, stepping down into the cargo hold.

Ty sat and watched from his seat. He opened the window and raised his hand to the Army captain standing near the elders. The elders waved back at him. Smiling a little, Ty felt good about what they were doing here. Every Afghan village who had seen help, food, antibiotics and support appreciated their presence. The Special Forces teams kept the Taliban out of the villages so that they could get on with their planting and harvest. They would have enough food for the winter months instead of starvation stalking them. Life out here, he felt, was tenuous at best.

He tried not to stare at Rachel but couldn't help himself as she stood out among his two crew members. The flight suit, although loose, still couldn't hide the fact that she was a woman. Her rounded hips gave her away. Ty liked the way she swayed when she walked. Rachel carried a load of boxes in her arms, even though she didn't have to carry anything. It told Hamilton she was a team player. With her helmet off, her dark brown hair glinted in the first rays of the sun edging over the peak and into the valley. He saw red and gold strands highlighted among her sable mane.

He got up and took his binoculars with him. As he strolled out of the rear of the bird, Hamilton continued to watch the slopes. No matter how good the men of this village had done their work, he never trusted the area was clear of clever Taliban. His job was to stay around the helo and keep it safe. Training his binoculars upward to the outpost, sitting on a flattened peak two thousand feet above them, Hamilton continued to hunt for enemy.

* * *

"Captain?" The Special Forces officer directed his focus to Rachel. She had just handed the paramedic in the group the medical supplies. Turning, she met the gray, narrowed gaze of the officer who commanded the team. He was easily over six feet tall, his head swathed in a dirty white-and-blue turban, his black beard scruffy. He was dressed like an Afghan man, as was the rest of his team, so they didn't stand out. His weapon hung off his broad shoulder. There was a sense of danger about this man, of a predator ready to spring.

"Captain Trayhern," she said, stopping in front of him.

"Welcome to our little slice of heaven," he said, giving her a tight grin. "I'm Captain Cain Morris."

"What can I do for you?" Rachel asked. She noticed the man's gaze was always moving across the slopes above the village. She felt safer.

"Tell Hamilton I've got the daughter of the village chief, and she needs immediate medical attention. She's only seventeen, very pregnant, and my paramedic, who's a man, can't see her, much less touch her. She's been bleeding the last three days."

Rachel saw the frustration in the captain's eyes. "That's not good. I'm not a paramedic, but even I know that."

"Yes. I've persuaded the elder to allow his daughter and his wife to fly back on your bird. You need to tell Hamilton that as soon as he drops off the cargo to the outpost above us, he has to make a beeline for the main Army base near Kabul. My paramedic says she's in real trouble, and so is the baby she's carrying. She's overdue."

Touched by the officer's concern, Rachel said, "I'll

call him and find out." She turned and walked away from the group. Hamilton had given her a radio to stay in touch with him. When he came on, she explained the situation. "What do I tell this captain?" she asked of Hamilton.

"Tell him to get the woman and the mother ready. We can't wait an hour here on the ground. They have to move pronto. The longer we're on the ground, the more we're a target. Tell Morris, ten minutes."

"Roger that." Turning, Rachel walked back to the captain. He nodded and quickly walked over to the dark, bearded man, who was in his fifties. Rachel was impressed that the captain spoke Pashto, the language of the area. The elder looked relieved and shouted orders. Immediately, two men ran down the dusty village road toward the rock homes.

Morris came back to Rachel. "I need you to stay here and wait for them. These people have never seen a helo before we came here, much less rode in one. I know the girl who's pregnant is very shy. Her mother will accompany her, but both can use your woman's touch."

"Sure, no problem," Rachel said, peering past his shoulder. A door opened and two women came out through it, dressed in black burkas, hidden from head to toe. It was obvious the shorter of the two was very pregnant.

Rachel had no time to dally. Once the women were on board, Hamilton was up front bringing the twin engines online. She smiled and patted the mother's hand. Both of them seemed frightened. Rachel just hoped the girl wouldn't deliver the baby here, in the back of the bird. She had no idea what to do to help her. Moving up front, she quickly got into the copilot's seat, pulled on her helmet and plugged the connection into the intercom system.

"Did you give those two earplugs?" Hamilton demanded, his hands flying across the instrument panel.

"Roger that," Rachel said, strapping in.

"You're taking us off. I'll direct you to the outpost and where to land."

Good, she had something to do. Gripping the cyclic and collective, she spoke to the crewmen in the back. The ramp was down, one of them manning the machine gun. Liftoff!

Flying to the outpost was a quick trip. The rotors raised thick, blinding clouds of yellow dust. Hamilton once more talked her down, and relief flooded through Rachel as she landed. In no time, the engines were shut down. This time, Hamilton leaped out of his seat.

"Stay here with the helo. And try to make these two women feel welcome. They look like they're going to bolt out of the rear."

Rachel removed her helmet. There was quick teamwork in the back. The Army soldiers from the outpost swarmed into the rear of the Chinook, helping the other three get the boxes off-loaded as quickly as possible. She stepped down and went to the two Afghan women. They looked positively frightened. Kneeling down in front of them, one hand on each of their hands, Rachel tried to soothe them. Her Pashto was rough at best, but trying to speak it made both of them appear relieved.

Within two minutes, the bird's cargo bay was cleared. Rachel divided her attention between the frightened women and the men smiling and laughing at the rear of the helo. When she saw Hamilton stride back into the chopper, she rose. Giving the women one final smile, Rachel left and went to her copilot seat.

Hamilton's body brushed against her shoulder as he came and sat down. The space between the two seats was very narrow. Her flesh tingled where he'd accidentally grazed her. Trying to ignore the sensation, Rachel did as ordered and took off once the engines were online. In no time, they were airborne. Hamilton was on the radio with Camp Bravo telling them they were detouring to Bagram Air Base outside of Kabul.

Relieved that Bravo Command gave them permission to fly the two Afghan women directly to Bagram, Rachel felt lighter. Happier. She loved change. And today, a mundane and unexciting flight had turned into something much more. As she headed the helo up to eight thousand and pointed the nose of it toward Kabul, she heard Hamilton chuckle. She turned her head toward him for a moment and saw that he was smiling. How handsome he was. Even though she couldn't see half his face, hidden by the dark visor, she definitely noticed his mouth. Nearly hypnotized by it for a moment, Rachel shook off the sudden desire that bloomed within her. What was going on? Hamilton was her enemy. He had always been that. Confused, she stuck to flying the Chinook through the early morning air.

"A good day," Hamilton told her later. They had just landed at Bravo Camp. At 10:00 a.m., the sun and air were warming up. The Ops area was busy and frantic, as always. Two Apaches had just landed and another two were trundling out to take off. Noise from the blades of two other Chinooks filled the air, making it nearly impossible to hear conversations.

Rachel had her helmet bag, her clipboard and other flight gear in her left hand. Yes, it had been a good day, but she wasn't about to let Hamilton know that. When she lifted her hand to push through the door of Ops, Hamilton beat her to it. He shoved it open and stood aside.

Shocked by his gentlemanly gesture, Rachel nodded awkwardly and shouldered past him. She was glad to be at the Ops desk since she knew the drill from there. A sergeant handed her a flight mission form. Without looking back, she chose one of the small rooms. She entered and shut the door in order to focus on the report. Only this time, Hamilton followed her inside.

Turning, Rachel placed her gear on the floor next to the picnic table that doubled as a desk. "I'm sure I can fill out a report by myself," she said.

Ty sat down opposite her. "When you're flying an Apache, your report is very different from ours," he said quietly, not wanting to face the hardness he saw in her face. Damn, she was so good-looking, and yet, that icy demeanor made him smart inwardly. Ty reminded himself he was to blame for her defensiveness. "Sit down." He opened one of his flight pockets and pulled out two pieces of folded paper. "When we fly, we have to name the outpost, village or any other items that may be important for Intelligence. This morning, we landed at a village whose name you don't know and can't spell as yet." He opened the papers and nudged one of them toward her. "I made a copy of all the villages, names of elders and outposts that we normally service. In your report, you need to not only put in the names and places but how we also transported two women to Bagram."

It made sense to Rachel. Still, she didn't like Hamilton sitting across from her. Taking the pen from her pocket, she looked down at the neatly typed list. Hamilton might be a sonofabitch, but he was thorough.

Rachel saw the names of villages, the elders' names, their wives' and children's names, the outposts. "This looks very complete," she said.

The softening in her voice made him relax a little. Giving her a slight smile, he said, "I learned a long time ago flying over here that if I didn't know the names, I couldn't connect with the people."

"No," Rachel murmured, studying the list, "you get a lot further if you know the name of a village's leader."

"Right," Ty said. He reached over and pointed to the paper. "Captain Morris supplied the name of the daughter. The wife is on this list."

Dutifully, Rachel filled out her report. She had to have help from Hamilton several times regarding the list. Her Pashto wasn't that good, and she needed to get better at it. Suddenly, a question popped out of her. "Do you know Pashto?"

Surprised, Ty sat up. "Yes, I do. Well," he added, opening his hands, "I learned it over time. I've never taken an immersion course."

Rachel cursed herself for veering into personal territory. He didn't deserve anything from her. Angry with herself, she lowered her gaze back to her report, mouth thinned.

Heartened that she was showing at least a little interest, Ty added, "You know, we have a Rosetta Stone version on Pashto here at the squadron. If you're interested, you can use it and bone up on the language a little more in your spare time."

Rachel said nothing. She signed off on the report, turned it around. "I'm assuming you'll read this, and if there are any corrections, your clerk will let me know."

Ty glanced up as she stood, grabbed her gear and got ready to leave. "Yes, I will."

"I'll find out when I fly again out at the Ops desk," she said, her voice firm as she opened the door.

Ty sat there alone in the room, the door closing once more. For a moment, the room had been warm. Alive. But now it was sterile once more. He did his best to continue with his report. His heart ached, and he had the feeling it wasn't physical. Rubbing his chest, Ty tried to figure out why things had suddenly changed. Frustrated, he tried again to focus on his report.

The more he tried to work, the more flashes of Rachel's face, her beautiful gold eyes haunted him. He'd seen the gentleness in her expression when she'd brought the two frightened women into the helo. He'd felt his heart respond when she'd smiled and patted their hands to try and relieve their fear. Like the starving wolf that he was, Ty had found himself wishing she was looking at him like that. And touching him intimately...

"Crazy, dude," he muttered darkly as he forced himself back to his paperwork. "Certifiably crazy..." Once, he'd hated her so much he was blinded by it. Now five years had passed. He'd grown and maybe matured a little. So what the hell was this emotional response to Rachel? Ty looked up, sighed and stared around the quiet room. The worst part, he was saddled with her at close quarters for the next six months.

Chapter 6

The sun had just risen as Rachel stood with the three other women from the Black Jaguar Squadron. It was freezing, and she was glad to have on her heavy green coat and gloves. Today, Hamilton would train them on cargo net hauling and delivery. He'd ordered them to meet him at the other end of the airstrip where a Chinook was standing by. What got her curious was a wooden pole about ten feet high, anchored into a bunch of sand bags. What was Hamilton up to now?

"Today," Ty told the huddled group of women pilots, "you're going to practice delivering cargo to outposts. As you know, all outposts are perched on the highest peak they can find. Those ten-man squads are cut off from normal supply routes. No one can climb those rocky mountains." He patted the thick, round pole. "So, what we do is we use two huge cargo nets. My crews will fill them with boxes of ammunition, medical supplies and MREs, meals ready to eat." He walked over to where the two cargo nets were lying on the tarmac. Picking one up, he elaborated, "These are not the normal nets you might be thinking of. They're made of steel cable that has been woven together. They are designed to carry a lot of weight. And the weight will be different on every flight. Each outpost sends in a weekly order to the Ops desk. The ground crews collect it, and then on a given day, we fly it out to them."

Rachel tried to ignore how handsome Hamilton was in front of the group. She recalled flight school and his arrogant, intimidating style of teaching. He wasn't doing it here. Instead, he was open, educational and actually nonthreatening. A far cry from five years ago. She wrapped her arms against her chest, the high-altitude cold stealing her warmth.

Ty dropped the thick, heavy cargo netting onto the tarmac and straightened. "Today we'll be practicing cargo drops and cargo pickups until you get them right and feel comfortable doing them. This pole is here for a reason. You're going to have a very small area to gently put those two huge cargo nets near the outpost. You won't be able to land. Instead, you're going to listen to your load master, who will be near the opening where they're hooked up. He'll guide you down to six feet above the ground. At six feet, they're on the ground. Then you have to hold this helo perfectly still so the load master can unhook them." He looked at each of their serious faces. Ty wanted to stare moments longer at Rachel but didn't.

"Okay," Rachel spoke up, "so we hover."

"Right," Ty said. "But you need to be aware of something. First, when those two cargo hooks are released, there are two men down under the belly of this helo."

He pointed to the CH-47. "Secondly, you can't allow mountain winds or currents to push this bird around. One small error, and you could crush these two soldiers who are under the helo. They're trying to get the cargo nets out from beneath it as fast as they can. Then once they've dragged the nets clear, four other men will quickly open them up and form a line to take the crates out of them."

Rachel withheld comment as he became deadly serious. Why did he have to have such a beautifully shaped male mouth? It would be so much easier if Hamilton were ugly, and then she could blatantly ignore him.

"Now, here's the tricky part," he told them. Using his left hand to illustrate, he said, "Here's the landing zone." He held his other hand barely above the left one. "Here you are with a heavy transport helo that is bucking local or regional mountain winds. You must hover there until they can refill these nets with empty cartridge and ammo cases, their trash and whatever else needs to go back to the base camp."

"So," Rachel said, "those men are dragging these nets back up under the helo?"

Nodding, Ty smiled a little. Rachel's cheeks were flushed, while everyone else seemed cold. "Exactly. You have two men struggling with the weight of those cargo nets. And they're risking their lives by once more, pulling them under the belly of our bird. The load master is hovering just above them, his hand stretched out to try and get one hook and then the other. This is a very delicate ballet between ground and flight personnel. The key is keeping the helo rock-solid steady during this time. Outpost drops and pickups are the hardest parts of flying out here on the frontier."

There was a murmur among the four women Apache pilots.

Ty walked over to the pole and wrapped his hand around it. "I know in an Apache, you don't do this type of flying, so none of you are really accustomed to this situation. That's why we're out here today. We're going to spend it taking the Chinook up and then hovering. You'll be working via communications with the load master. We'll hook up these two cargo nets with a lot of weight. Your job is to slowly lower the helo until this pole almost touches the belly of the helo. That is exactly how many feet you have. If you come in too fast, you'll splinter the pole. And if that had been real, that pole was a soldier waiting under the belly of your helo to get the netting released. You have just badly injured or killed him."

Rachel traded grim stares with the other women pilots.

"And then I'll have two crewmen standing by, out of range, as you bring and hover the bird just above that pole. Today, you're going to learn to trust your load master's direction and follow his orders exactly. Further, you need to learn to handle the bulk of this helo, feel the sudden loss of all that cargo weight and then the sudden addition to it. There will be a lot of bobbling up and down when that happens, and you can't allow it. You can crush the men beneath you."

"Wow, a real dance," Rachel muttered under her breath. Her brows drew down. She realized instantly that they all had a long way to go on learning this maneuver. Seeing the worry in the faces of every pilot, she knew they all got the seriousness of the training.

Ty looked over the women. "Any questions?" He saw all of them shake their heads. "Okay, then let's get going. I'm going to be sitting in the left-hand seat, and you'll each be the pilot in command. You'll have to get used to doing it from one side of the helo and the other. If you're right-handed, it's always easier to do it from the right seat. We'll build your confidence there, and then we'll transfer you to the left seat. Most pilots have a weak and strong side when they fly. You'll find out pretty quickly where that's at." He managed a slight grin.

He pointed to Rachel, "Okay, you're first, Captain Trayhern. Let's saddle up."

Great. Rachel scowled but didn't say anything. When Hamilton was her flight instructor back at Fort Rucker, he would always yell at her, curse her and tell her how bad a flyer she was. Would he do that now? God, she hoped not because she would land the damned helo and go to Ops and report him for harassment.

Joining Hamilton, she kept her distance from his shoulder. The sun felt good, the temperature only slightly higher. The rest of the base was still busy, like bees coming and going. Apaches were warming up for takeoff. Two Chinooks bearing two cargo nets beneath their bellies slowly lifted into the air, bound for outposts in the godforsaken brown mountains.

As Rachel climbed into the helo, she saw that Sergeant Tony Bail was standing near the big, square opening in the middle of the belly of the chopper. He raised his hand and smiled. Rachel nodded to him. This twenty-year-old would be giving her directions. She took her helmet out of the bag and pulled it on. Hamilton waited for her to climb the stairs. Heart pounding, Rachel quickly moved to the pilot's right-hand seat. She concentrated on their preflight list and then engaged the rear and front rotors.

"Okay," Hamilton told her, pulling his microphone close to his mouth, "let's take her up and go to five hundred feet. From there, I want you to pretend we're over an outpost. You'll have those cargo slings under you. You'll feel the load. Ready?"

"I am," Rachel said, hand around the collective and cyclic. Her boots were firm on the rudders beneath her feet. The shaking and shuddering of the helo soothed her nerves. Rachel tried to steel herself against a potential tirade from her new boss and old enemy. Lifting off, they broke connection with the earth. Instantly, as she slowly pulled the helo upward without tipping forward or back, Rachel felt the tremendous weight of the slings. She responded to it.

"Good ascent," Ty said.

Relief sped through her for a moment. Was that praise? Rachel said nothing, climbing to five hundred feet and hovering.

"Okay," Ty said, "begin to lower. Sergeant, take over?"

"Yes, sir. Okay, ma'am, I'm down on my knees near the opening. I will talk you down."

"Roger," Rachel said. She knew the other three women pilots were watching. Nerves taut, she began to ease the Chinook down.

"Your nose is high," Ty warned.

As she glanced quickly at the horizon indicator, Rachel noticed he was right. Not by much. Okay, he was going to be a stickler on a flat landing where nose and tail were exactly even. Correcting, she watched the altimeter slowly unwind. Bail's voice was high and nasal, but he was good at direction.

"Continue lowering," he told her.

Rachel lived in fear of striking that upright pole. As they got closer, sweat popped out on her upper lip.

"Twenty feet," Bail warned her. "A little slower..."

It was a delicate dance. Rachel's hands gripped the controls hard. She was constantly using her rudders to keep the helo from swinging one way or another as she continued the descent.

"Fifteen feet, keep coming..."

The winds across the base were always around. A gust hit the bird.

"Too fast!" Bail yelled.

Gulping, Rachel tried to recover from the gust. Suddenly, she heard the load master give a yelp.

"Ascend!" Hamilton ordered.

Instantly, Rachel applied power.

"Hover at one hundred feet and hold," he ordered her.

What had happened? Rachel saw Hamilton craning his neck over the seat and looking into the cargo hold.

"Ma'am," the load master said, his voice tight, "you just destroyed the pole. The bottom of the helo nearly got impaled on it."

"Roger that," Rachel said, feeling ashamed.

She looked over at Hamilton, expecting him to scream at her. Instead, to her shock, he appeared calm. "Is there another pole?"

"Yes, we have plenty of them." One corner of his mouth pulled upward. "Not to worry. We destroy plenty of them in this exercise."

Rachel winced. "If that had been a man under there..."

"He'd be dead," Hamilton finished, becoming somber.

"It was the wind."

"It's always going to be wind and air currents," he told her. "That's your biggest enemy in this exercise."

Nodding, Rachel looked out the right window. Below, she could see two crewmen taking the broken pole out from the sandbags and replacing it with another one. She gave Hamilton a quick glance, feeling on her guard. He wasn't screaming. No curses. Instead, a quiet kind of instruction. Rachel inhaled deeply. "Sergeant, tell me when that pole is up."

"Yes, ma'am. It's up and we're ready to try again."

"Okay, I'm coming in. Begin direction, Sergeant."

Ty said nothing. He saw the tension in Rachel's beautifully shaped mouth. A mouth he had a damned hard time not watching like a lovesick puppy. Why hadn't he been aware of her beauty back in flight school? Giving an internal shake of his head, Ty concentrated on her skills. She was obviously nervous and wanting to do it right. He'd learned the hard way that yelling at a student didn't bring out their best. All it did was increase tension and cause more errors in flying.

Rachel listened to the sergeant as he talked her down. This time, even though the wind was inconstant and trying to push the helo around, she held it steady. It was so different from the nimble, super-powered Apache.

"Stop and hover!" the sergeant called, his voice rising.

Instantly, Rachel held the hover. They must have been directly over the pole. She heard the load master breathing hard. It took a lot of pure muscle to get those hooks removed.

"Continue hover," Bail called.

"Roger," she murmured, praying that the wind would hit them.

And it did. One moment, Rachel was static. The next, the gust of wind hit the helo and they started to slide.

"Up! Up!" Bail yelled.

She cursed softly under her breath, her feet and hands moving at incredible speed. The Chinook was thrown sideways and started to skid. The ground was only twenty feet away, and she saw it come up fast. Instantly, she powered the helo and rose. Her heart pounded in her chest like it would jump out. Not a word from Hamilton.

As she brought the Chinook into a hover at a hundred feet, Rachel cast a quick glance in his direction. His face was unreadable, but his blue eyes were narrowed. Licking her lips, she felt shaky inside, as if she were a new pilot, not the veteran that she was.

"Nice recovery," Hamilton told her. "Take it easy. Everyone is going to do exactly what you're doing. This isn't a case of trying to look good, Captain Trayhern. It's learning the ropes. You're going to make a lot of mistakes today, so get over it."

Trembling inwardly, Rachel felt her gut twist into a literal knot. She had always wanted to do things perfectly, without messing up. But she was doing it big time this morning. What did her friends, her sister pilots, think of her screwups? Ashamed, Rachel focused even harder on the task.

"Okay," Ty said, "let's try again. You're getting better every time you do it. That's as good as it gets." He saw the pain and shame in the way her mouth twisted. The shield was down over her eyes, so he couldn't see them. Didn't matter. He knew from a lot of experience that every pilot made the same mistakes. Even he did.

* * *

The sun was setting as Rachel made her way to the Ops room to fill out her report. The other female pilots had followed her off the tarmac to their individual rooms. Once inside, Rachel closed her eyes and scrubbed her face.

"What a sucky day," she muttered, walking over to the table and sitting down. The room was quiet. A report had to be filed. Right now, all she wanted was a stiff jolt of tequila, her favorite drink when she could get it. Her gut was still tight, especially knowing that Hamilton was making his way through the four rooms. She was sure he'd be here sooner or later. Rachel ran her fingers through her loose hair and pulled the pen out of the upper-arm pocket of her flight suit.

Rachel was almost done with her report when the door opened. Hamilton stepped in, carrying two mugs of coffee. Shutting the door with his boot, he turned and said, "I figured you'd need a stiff cup of coffee about right now."

Rachel straightened. She wasn't sure how to contain her surprise. Without thinking, she took the cup from him. The instant their fingertips met, she felt the tingle. Unable to jerk her hand away, she took the cup and said, "You're right about that."

Ty walked around the table and sat down opposite her. He made sure his knees didn't touch hers. There was wariness in her face as always. "The other pilots finished their reports. I brought them coffee, too, because I know how nerve-racking this training is."

Rachel took a sip of the hot brew. "I don't know why I didn't think to get some coffee earlier. My nerves are shot."

"Understandable."

"That's some of the toughest, most demanding flying I've ever done," she admitted, signing off on the report.

"I know. And flying an Apache you have to be a multitasker, but this is different."

Rachel nodded. She wrapped her hands around the mug as he picked up her printed report and read it. Inspector pilots and flight instructors had to sign off on their students' reports. Rachel stared at Hamilton's face as he read. It gave her a moment to simply study him. Again, she wished he wasn't so damned handsome. He had a strong nose and chin, his cheekbones high. As her gaze settled on his mouth, Rachel suddenly felt heat in her lower body. She scowled. She shouldn't have any reaction to this man.

Ty looked up and caught her staring at him. Rachel suddenly glanced away. For a brief second, he'd seen something else in her golden eyes. Always, there was wariness and distrust in them when he was around. But not this time. What did he see? It was so quick, he didn't have time to register it. Rachel appeared very uncomfortable, squirming around on the bench. Why? He was doing his level best not to be a torment to her as he'd been before. He wanted her to know that he had no wish to take on the Trayherns again. Burned by past experience, Ty wanted the rest of his career to go without rancor.

"Good report," he congratulated her.

Rachel smiled uneasily as she placed the mug on the table. "Brutally frank as always."

"Well," Ty murmured, adding some sentences to the bottom of it, "you're too hard on yourself."

"I should have gotten the swing of things sooner," she muttered.

"You got it faster than the other three pilots. That should make you feel good."

Hamilton's voice was soothing and unperturbed. It was such a diametric difference from her last experience with him at flight school. "I guess," she said.

"I wish I could erase that look in your eyes," Ty said, frowning.

Rachel sat up a little more. "What look?"

Ty sighed and signed off on the report and handed it back to her. "Distrust."

Shocked, she glared at him. "Well, given our past, Captain Hamilton, do you blame me?"

Her voice was gritty. Scathing. Ty felt his shoulders tense. His heart beat a little harder over her sudden combativeness. Holding up his hands, he said, "Look, I know we have a bad past history."

"That's not the half of it," Rachel growled.

"I understand," he said, trying to speak softly so as to defuse the animosity in the room.

Rising, Rachel stared down at him, feeling all her fear and tension unwinding within her. "No, you don't. I had you screaming in my face, cursing me and threatening me for twelve weeks solid. No one would ever forget that, Captain Hamilton." She put the mug down on the table a little too roughly, some of the coffee spilling out of it. "I'll never forget what you did to me. And frankly, I'm just waiting for that mask of yours to come off and you to go after me again." Her cheeks grew hot as she hurled those words at him. He appeared positively thunderstruck.

Ty sat there for a moment, digesting the cold rage in her voice. She had her hands on her hips, leaning forward like the aggressive Apache combat pilot she was.

But there was fear in the depths of her narrowed eyes—of him. She still feared him. There was no trust.

Those realizations hit him hard. Ty tried to find the right words. But who could under the circumstances? "Look, I know I screwed up with you. I've paid a fair price for it, and I accept my demotion and the fact I'll never be let into the Apache club again. I've been trying to show you that I won't be like that now. I've learned my lesson, Captain Trayhern."

Anger roared through her bloodstream. Rachel felt herself trembling with the long-held rage. "The last place I ever want to be is in your company. I might have to put up with you for six months, but that's it. Am I dismissed, Captain Hamilton?"

Actual physical pain moved through Ty's heart. He slowly stood, staring across the table at Rachel. She was so incredibly beautiful, her brown hair shining around her and emphasizing her gold eyes. He hesitated. There was so much he wanted to say, but she wouldn't hear or believe it. Finally, he rasped, "Dismissed, Captain Trayhern. I'll see you here for a flight at 0600 tomorrow."

Turning on her heel, Rachel fairly ran out of the room. Ran and got the hell away from Hamilton. Boots thunking across the wooden floor, Rachel jerked the door open, slammed it shut and took off.

The room fell silent. Ty looked around it, the report still on the table in front of him. His conscience ate at him. Now, he was seeing what his hatred of women five years earlier had done to Rachel. Shaking his head, he scooped up the report. Her disgust of him was clearly written in her eyes. As he walked to the door and opened it, Hamilton couldn't blame her. He'd been a real bastard back then. Prejudicial, stupid, backward and letting his own childhood color his perception of women in general. Well, now he had another war to fight. With Rachel Trayhern. As he walked toward the Ops desk, the place busy as always, Ty felt depressed. He'd wounded a beautiful, smart, courageous woman who had no connection with his earlier life. And yet, he'd taken it all out on her. How could he get her to trust him?

Chapter 7

Rachel woke up in a very bad mood. On her way over to Ops to meet Hamilton, she barely acknowledged the pink sky flooding the eastern horizon before the sun peeked over the mountain range. Gripping her helmet bag, she moved through the streams of people coming and going to morning duties. How could she have dreamed of kissing Hamilton? Of all things! And it had been so real Rachel had awakened in the early morning hours feeling an ache in her lower body.

Oh, she knew that ache. Why wasn't Garrett in her dream instead? She'd loved him with her life until he'd died in an attack on the Apache base Camp Alpha in Helmand Province a year earlier. But to be kissing Hamilton? Rolling her eyes, Rachel tried to shove that heated dream down into the basement of her memory. She had to focus on the coming helo mission with Hamilton.

As she entered Ops, the familiar rush and buzz of Apache pilots was in high gear. As soon as it was light enough, the transport squadron would become active. Unlike the Apache pilots, the CH-47 had no nighttime flight capability. It was a basic, utilitarian helo that flew only during the day and in good weather conditions. Apaches had the state-of-the-art gear for flying day and night and under any conditions. How badly Rachel missed flying her gun-ship.

She went to her cubbyhole and dragged out the mission orders for the day. She didn't see Hamilton and was glad for that small blessing.

"Hey, Captain Trayhern," the Ops sergeant called, "you've got goats today." He grinned.

Walking up to the balding sergeant, Rachel set the helmet bag at her feet and opened the orders. "Goats?"

"Yes, ma'am. They just flew in a cargo hold full of goats just a few minutes ago from Bagram. You and Captain Hamilton are taking them to Samarigam, a village real close to the Pakistan border."

As she read the orders, Rachel managed a wry smile. "Goats. Of all things."

"Ever transport them?" he asked, handing her a pen.

Shaking her head, Rachel laughed and said, "No, I haven't."

"Not something an Apache pilot has to deal with," he joked.

Rachel signed off on the orders and couldn't stop herself from smiling. *Goats.*

"Your bird is to the left of the doors. Crews are moving the crates of goats into it right now. Have fun!"

Lifting her hand, Rachel said, "Right."

Pushing out the doors of Ops, she saw the CH-47 she would be flying. Sure enough, just as the Ops sergeant had promised, there was maximum activity around the opened ramp of the CH-47 that had just flown in. They had specialized equipment to lift pallets out of the helos. Only this time, as she drew near, they were lifting pallets that contained groups of goats in crates.

Rachel watched the transfer as it went smoothly from one Chinook to the other. *Goats.* Who knew? The two crewmen for her helo were busy as she walked up the ramp and made her way to the cockpit. Up ahead, Hamilton was in the left-hand seat, clipboard on his thigh, writing. Her smile disappeared.

"Goats?" she asked, stepping up into the cockpit.

Ty looked up and removed his legs from the aisle so she could sit in the left-hand seat. "Morning," he murmured. Giving her a quick look, he noted there was no anxiety or anger in her eyes. She was breathtaking. "Yes," he said as she sat down and got comfortable in the seat, "this is a special mission we've been handed."

"I'll bet," Rachel said wryly. "The Ops sergeant told me we were hauling goats. We must be blessed by the higher-ups at the Pentagon."

"Oh," Ty said, finishing off his paperwork, "not just any goats. Angora goats. And this assignment did come down from the Pentagon."

Unable to stop grinning, Rachel took her helmet out of the bag. "Angora goats? As in mohair sweaters?"

Chuckling, Hamilton warmed inwardly. It was the first time he'd seen Rachel smile. And his heart took off at a strong beat. He watched hungrily as she threaded her fingers through her shining, straight brown hair and gathered it up and tied it back with a rubber band. "Yes. The U.S. Army is working with Captain Kahlid Shaheen on this project."

"Oh?" Rachel turned, interested. "Are Emma and Kahlid going to be up at that village?"

"Actually, yes," he said. "We'll be meeting them at Samarigam."

Her whole day was turning out to be better than expected. "That's great."

"She's your cousin, right?"

"Yes." Rachel saw some anxiety in Hamilton's blue eyes. She felt as if he were trying to make up for causing her explosion yesterday in the report room. She wouldn't apologize for her sharp words. Still, a bit of guilt ate at Rachel because it was sorely obvious that Hamilton was doing his best to be friendly, attentive and engaged. And then she remembered that torrid dream last night and gulped hard.

"I talked to the captain who flew the goats in from Kabul. Apparently, the farm program of Shaheen's organization has gotten the go ahead from the Pentagon and they're bringing in Angora goats to certain villages. And then they get the women who have been widowed to create a cooperative where they shear the goats and make sweaters from the mohair. It not only improves the village on a financial line, but widows aren't starving and dying, either."

"Emma had told me that Kahlid was working to get that project off the ground. It's a great one." Rachel was all too familiar with what happened to an Afghan wife who lost her husband to the ongoing war. Poverty was so severe in Afghanistan that when the husband died, the widow was then shunned. They were supposed to be taken in by the husband's family, but that rarely happened. Each family was barely subsisting off the land or the goat and sheep herds they had. The widows then had to go house-to-house every day, begging for scraps of food to keep them and their children alive.

"Well," Ty said, gloating, "we're the first official shipment of Angora goats. Just call us the Angora Express."

Pulling on her helmet, she grinned. "Somehow, Angora goats won't impress anyone who reads my personnel jacket."

Ty chuckled and pulled on his own helmet. "I hear you." The bleating of the goats rose as more of the crates were brought in. The crew members knew how to get as many in as they could. Once the last crate arrived, he saw his load master work with the other crewmen and pull a huge, thick nylon net around all of them. That way, the crates would be strapped to the deck, and if they hit turbulence or had to take evasive action, the crates wouldn't be flying around inside the helo.

Rachel's mood lightened considerably. She would see Emma and Kahlid, an unexpected and pleasant surprise. It made the two hours they'd be flying less arduous. As she twisted around in her seat and looked at the thickly woolen Angora goats, she had to smile. In one crate stood three big rams with long, twisted horns. The rest of the crates contained ewes, who had much smaller horns. They weren't terribly big in Rachel's opinion. But what did she know about goats?

"We're getting Apache escort today," Ty said, plugging his helmet connection into the radio system. He turned and gave the signal that the ramp was coming up. The goats were secure, and the men stood away from the ramp area.

"I saw that on the orders," she said. "I'm assuming you've done the walk around?"

"Done and we're looking good," he answered.

"Roger." For whatever reason, Rachel felt calm in the cockpit. Usually, she was tense, especially with Hamilton next to her. Today was different. Was it that stupid, ridiculous dream? Rachel shook her head and pulled out the preflight information. There was a working ease between them, which hadn't happened before. Maybe yesterday's verbal explosion had cleared the air. She certainly felt better letting Hamilton know just where she stood.

The bleating of the Angora goats was drowned out as Rachel brought the first engine and then the second one online. To her left, she saw an Apache trundling up, fully loaded with weapons. How Rachel wished she was over there and not here!

"Goat One to Goat Two," she called to the Apache.

"Goat Two here..." The woman pilot gave a "baaahhhhhh" over the radio.

Rachel broke into laughter. She glanced over at Hamilton, who was laughing, too. How handsome he looked when he smiled. She couldn't ever remember seeing him laugh. Then again, she had no business noticing him. She devoted her attention to talking with her friend, Nike. "Hey, you got goats over in Greece, doncha?"

"Roger that, Goat One," Nike snickered. "Over."

"Well, good to have this goat jamboree all working together. Nice to have you along, Nike. Over."

"Roger that, Goat One. Is your cargo looking happy about all this? Over."

"Negative, Goat Two." Rachel twisted around and looked at the crates beneath the thick cargo netting. It was barely light in the hold, but she could see them. "They're looking pretty wild-eyed. Over."

"Goat One, do you think someone with a sense

of humor picked today's call sign? Over." Nike was chuckling.

Hamilton's grin widened. "Goat One to Goat Two. Roger that. I'm to blame. Over."

Rachel smiled to herself as her hands flew over the instruments with knowing ease before they were to take off. She hadn't ever seen Hamilton's sense of humor, but she liked it.

"Goat One, you are the man! Over."

Nodding, Ty glanced over at Rachel. She was still grinning. The iciness that always hovered in the cockpit between them had miraculously disappeared. He ardently absorbed the warmth between them, finally tearing his gaze from Rachel's soft features.

"Goat Two, we're ready to get this goat train airborne. You ready to take off first? Over."

"Roger that, Goat One. We're outta here. Meet you at six thousand feet," Nike said. And then she added, "Baaahhhhhhh…"

Rachel laughed uproariously. "Roger that, Goat Two. See you upstairs. Out."

Ty sat back. Happiness thrummed through him. And relief. In no time, after the Apache had rolled down the airstrip, gathering speed and finally lifting off at the end of it, it was their turn. The CH-47 shook and shuddered. The thunderous roar of the engines was muted by their helmets. Ty looked back to see how the goats were dealing with the rolling take-off. They seemed to have quieted down.

Once airborne and at flight altitude, Rachel was happy to have the Apache flying a large circle around them. She knew Nike and her copilot had on infrared to spot heat from bodies down on the rugged mountain slopes. They also had instruments to detect a SAM missile being fired. She relaxed as never before because the Apache was the big, bad guard dog in the sky.

"I was wondering if you ever have been around goats," Ty asked Rachel over the intercom.

Smiling a little as she flew, Rachel said, "No. I grew up with aquariums of fresh-water and salt-water fish. My father loves fish."

"I grew up in Cheyenne, Wyoming where my parents owned a cattle ranch."

Rachel found herself curious about Hamilton. She knew nothing of him. And the two-hour flight would go faster if they had a conversation. "So, you're a cowboy?"

Chuckling, he said, "Yeah, among many other things. When you grow up on a ranch, you do everything from digging postholes, setting new fence, to stringing barbed wire, milking cows and fixing ranching equipment."

Somehow, Rachel hadn't ever thought of Hamilton as anything but the screaming flight instructor. Now, this presented a whole new facet of him. "I wasn't around too many animals. Just the fish—and Polly, my mother's beautiful parrot. Not a very creative name, but I grew up with Polly. No cattle, though."

"We had milk goats," Ty hesitantly admitted, filing away Rachel's information. He felt starved to make a human connection with her, one that wasn't filled with anger and dredging up their past. "My mother had the goats because they provided milk for children who were lactose intolerant and couldn't drink cows' milk."

"I'll bet she had you out there milking them," Rachel said. At least his mother sounded like a nice and thoughtful person. So how had Hamilton turned out to be so...complicated?

"I don't really remember the goats too much," he admitted in a quieter tone. "My mom died of uterine cancer when I was three years old. My dad got rid of the goats shortly after that."

Her heart plummeted over that information. Glancing quickly to her left, she saw him become sad and withdrawn. She wondered how he handled growing up without a mother. She couldn't imagine losing her mother, Kit. That would have been a horrible sentence for him to bear as a three-year-old. "I'm sorry to hear that," she murmured, meaning it. When she saw him nod, his mouth pursed, Rachel realized that he still missed her. Who wouldn't miss their mother?

"How did your father cope?" Rachel asked.

Hamilton shrugged. "It wasn't pretty. Looking back on it all, I don't think many men can lose their wife and then be saddled with a three-year-old kid."

The incredible grief in his voice startled her. The visor was drawn over the upper half of his face, so she couldn't see the expression in his eyes. The corners of his mouth were drawn in, no doubt sealing in his pain. Some of her hatred of him dissolved just knowing this past history. "I'm really sorry to hear that," Rachel admitted. And she was. Abandonment could have played a huge part in his growing-up years. She could only imagine the impact her death must have had on him.

Trying to rein in her curiosity, she asked, "Did your father remarry?" If he had, Hamilton would have at least had a stepmother figure in his life.

Hamilton gave an abrupt laugh, one tinged with bitterness. "No. He was a mean son of a bitch, and all he cared about was the family name and carrying on the hundred-and-fifty-year-old ranch tradition of our family."

Rachel cringed. She heard the sudden hardness, the yearning in Hamilton's tone. "Did you have brothers? Sisters?"

"No, I was their first and only child."

Rachel moistened her lips. She continued to rubberneck and watch sky and ground, just as Hamilton was doing. More sets of eyes meant less chance of the Taliban firing at them without being seen first. "It must have been tough as an only child, then," she suggested.

"Let's just say that my father didn't like a crying little boy who had suddenly lost his mother."

"He was grieving just like you, I'm sure," Rachel said, hoping to ease the hurt she heard. "When you love someone and suddenly lose them… Well, it's hard. Really hard." She knew better than most, too.

"Let's put it this way, Captain Trayhern. My father blamed me for my mother's death. Oh, looking back on it now, he was wrong, but when you're a little kid, you believe your parent."

"That's wrong! You didn't cause her cancer," Rachel whispered fervently.

Giving her a glance, Ty heard and felt her compassion. Her soft lips were parted. In that moment, he ached to crawl into her arms and simply be held. It was such a startling thought that he sat up a little straighter. What was going on here? There was no way Rachel would ever like him. Hell, she hated him. And for good reason. Still, in that explosive moment of actually talking with one another, the need rose in him. He simply didn't know what to do with it. "Sure it was wrong," he mumbled.

"So you grew up being accused and reminded that your mom was dead because of you?" Rachel asked, disbelief in her voice.

"My father didn't accuse me of it daily. Only a couple of times…"

"What a lousy parent he was. You never saddle a child with something horrendous like that."

"My father continued to remind me that women were the weak species. They didn't have what it took to be strong and survive in this hard world of ours."

Stunned, Rachel tried to absorb that information. No wonder he had this prejudice against women. She knew she had to be careful with her words. "And you were young and believed him."

"Sure I did," Ty muttered. He lifted his hands in frustration. "I believed him body and soul until five years ago."

Wincing inwardly, Rachel suddenly wished they didn't have this mission. How badly she wanted to have time to understand the roots of Hamilton's actions. They had started with an angry, grieving father. And being the little boy he was, he'd believed his father. Women were weak because his wife had died of cancer. She'd left him with Ty, who was an innocent, grieving child. Gulping several times, Rachel fought the tears jamming into her eyes. She was grateful her visor was down and he couldn't see her face.

There was nothing she could say. His belief that women were weak had all come to a roaring halt when she'd fought back. And won. Had Hamilton really let go of his prejudice toward women? Was he really a changed man? After a week in his company, Rachel admitted that he wasn't anything like the strident flight instructor of five years earlier. Still, her heart warned her to remain on guard. Could someone who carried such an intolerance suddenly change?

"Ah, Goat Land ahead," Ty teased, trying to lighten

the atmosphere. He pointed ahead at a high mountain valley. "There's our village."

Rachel struggled for a moment before she could speak. When she did, her voice was oddly hoarse. "Goat Land? You've got a wicked sense of humor, Captain."

He glanced over and managed a smile. "Dark humor at best." Seeing her lower lip tremble, Ty felt his heart wrench in his chest. And then he saw the track of tears down her cheek. Her voice had been raspy, but he hadn't put it together until now. Crying. She was crying for *him.*

Chapter 8

Upon landing at Samarigam, Rachel was swept up in the village's excitement. To her surprise, Khalid and Emma had already flown in, their helo having landed nearby. They had transported in twenty bleating Angora goats. Some of her levity was dampened by the uneasiness that Hamilton had shared so much of himself with her. Now, she saw him differently.

"Go ahead and meet and greet," Hamilton urged her. "I'll work with the crew and the villagers to off-load these crates of goats."

Rachel nodded and quickly moved between the fuselage and crates. After placing a green scarf over her head to honor Muslim tradition, she eagerly walked down the ramp. Outside, the villagers had gathered, their faces alight with joy over receiving such an expensive gift from the United States. Threading through them, Rachel found Emma and Khalid at the corral with the elders. Before approaching them, she greeted the four old men, the elders, of the village. Protocols were important. They shook her hand and greeted her in return. Emma was smiling as Rachel came toward her.

"Hey, Cousin, look at this!" Emma threw her arms around Rachel and hugged her tightly. Releasing her, she laughed. "We did it!"

Rachel beamed at her. "You did. A dream come true." She turned to Khalid, who was still in the U.S. Army, wearing the flight uniform. His face lit up with pleasure. As Rachel moved to shake his hand, his arms went around her, and he hugged her.

"Welcome, Rachel," he said, releasing her.

"Thanks, Captain Shaheen," she said.

"Out here, call me Khalid. You're my family now. Let's drop Army protocols when we can, shall we?"

"Fine with me," Rachel said.

They led her over to the four-foot-high corral.

"This village will have forty-five Angora goats," Emma said excitedly. "Khalid and his sister Kinah have been working two years to make this dream into a reality."

Rachel saw that the rest of the villagers hung on the wooden fence, staring in disbelief at the white animals. The children were on their hands and knees, peeking between the slats, eyes wide with excitement. "This is a great day," she agreed. Khalid's arm went around Emma's shoulders and he hugged her, his face bright. "So, the widows get the wool to make sweaters?"

Emma nodded. "There are several surrounding villages to Samarigam. They're all the same clan. Khalid has a written contract agreement with the elders from six villages that the widows will receive the wool from these goats every year. Each woman will get enough to make ten sweaters."

"And then," Khalid said with a smile, "they will be sold through our nonprofit organization around the world. The widows receive seventy-five percent of the money. This will not only keep them from starvation, but it will also feed their children. No one will die. And the money the widows spend in their village on goods circulates through the local economy. It's a win-win for everyone."

Smiling, Rachel noted the joy in Khalid's expression. He was lean as a snow leopard, terribly handsome, and she was so happy for Emma. They were truly a happily married couple, who held the same vision for the people of Afghanistan. "That's incredible."

"We have Kinah to thank," Emma told her. "She's set up distribution through the U.S. for all the sweaters. And she has hired three women who will be coming here to teach the widows the patterns and how to knit them."

"You've thought of everything." Rachel looked at the goats moving around in the large, circular corral. The children had brought handfuls of green grass gathered from the hillside. The goats were settling down, anxious to eat.

"Here comes the rest of the herd," Khalid said, motioning to the village men hand carrying the crates off the Chinook.

Stepping aside, Rachel watched a long line of men struggling with each crate. The goats bleated, terrified as they were carefully carried. One by one, each crate was taken into the corral and the goats released. Upon finding their own kind already there, the animals lost their fright and eagerly crowded in to grab a few bits of grass offered by the children at the fence.

Overhead, an Apache flew in large circles around the village. It was searching for infrared signatures of human beings who could be Taliban in hiding. The enemy could lie in wait to lob a grenade at one of the two Chinooks on the ground. Craning her neck, Rachel saw the last crate leaving the ramp of her helo. Hamilton was standing by it. He was alert, looking around. It was never safe to be on the ground for long.

"How safe is Samarigam?" she asked Emma.

"Very safe. Khalid chose this village because the Taliban has not been here at all."

Khalid looked up at the Apache as it passed over them. He then glanced over at Rachel. "That doesn't mean it's safe flying here or back. It's Taliban country, big time."

"That's what I thought," Rachel said. She saw Hamilton gesturing for her to come back to the helo. "Excuse me, my boss is wanting to see me."

Hurrying through the happy crowd of villagers, who watched each release of the Angora goats, Rachel finally broke free of the people and noticed the worried expression on Hamilton's face.

"What's wrong?" she asked, coming up to him.

Hamilton looked in the cavernous hold of the helo. "Both our crewmen are sicker than dogs."

"What?" Alarmed, Rachel stepped onto the ramp. Both crewmen were sitting and looking very pale.

"They've been throwing up. A lot of nausea. I don't know why."

"Emma and Khalid are flying back to Bagram. A straight shot from here. We could ask them to take them to the hospital there."

"That's what I was thinking," Hamilton agreed. "Could be food poisoning. They both said they ate tuna sandwiches for breakfast this morning."

Rachel wrinkled her nose. "For breakfast? What a horrible thing to eat!" And there was a chow hall so everyone could get eggs and bacon. Shaking her head, she muttered, "Twenty-somethings..."

Hamilton smiled a little. "I'm going to call back to base and let Ops know. Since I'm the commander of the squadron, I can release them to Bagram and Khalid's helo."

"Good. You want me to tell Emma and Khalid? I'm sure they won't mind."

"Yes, can you?" He hesitated. "It leaves us open, though. We won't have a ramp gunner watching for the Taliban."

"I know," she said. "But they aren't going to be any good to us sick, either."

Nodding, Ty knew she was right. "Okay, you make sure it's okay with them, and I'll make the radio call to Camp Bravo."

Once she heard the situation, Emma shook her head. "These young guys are really dumb sometimes. Mayonnaise is a real lethal food-poisoning ingredient if it hasn't been chilled at the right temperature."

"Tell me about it," Rachel said.

"We'll take them to Bagram," Khalid said. "Just ask them to walk over and make themselves at home in our bird."

"Thanks," she told them. "We really appreciate this. Otherwise, we'd have to detour and fly a lot longer than we expected."

"Not to worry," Emma said, putting her hand on Rachel's shoulder. "The U.S. Army isn't going to say anything. They don't care if they're flown in a civilian Chinook or not." She grinned.

"Something nice about being a civilian, isn't there?" Rachel teased her red-haired cousin.

"Oh, yes." Emma smiled warmly up at her husband. "It's *very* nice."

Chuckling, Rachel waved goodbye to them and trotted back to their helo. Hamilton had just walked down the ramp when she approached the bird.

"Everything's in order," he told her.

Rachel said, "Good. Let's tell the guys to trade helos. They'll take them directly to the base hospital."

Ty nodded and walked inside. He told the sick crewmen what was going on. They slowly got up and walked down the ramp. He escorted them to the commercial Chinook helo that had the nonprofit name of the Shaheen's organization painted on it. The crewmen laid down on the nylon netting that served as seats on the helo.

Upon reaching his bird, he saw that Rachel had already gone up to the cockpit. She was talking on the radio.

Rachel turned and saw Hamilton coming up the stairs. She'd taken the left-hand seat to answer the radio call. He sat down, his expression curious. Finishing the call, she said, "Ops just called us. They're redirecting us to the Kabul River on the other side of the mountain and north of Peshuwar."

"Why?"

"The Kabul River is flooding due to heavy thunderstorms over the mountains. There's an anti-Taliban village that needs our help. People are trapped in the river and need to be rescued."

"Our Apache protection can't go with us. They've only got so much fuel," Hamilton said.

"I know. They have to head back and can't make that swing east to help, due to a low-fuel situation."

"Not good," Ty muttered. He looked around, thinking. "The Kabul River above Peshuwar is heavy Taliban country."

Rachel handed him the microphone. "You talk to Bagram HQ then. They're the ones ordering us to do it."

Taking the mike, Hamilton made a call into the headquarters. He argued that they shouldn't be risking their bird or lives without crewmen on board and without Apache escort, but he got no further than Rachel did. After clicking it off, Hamilton glanced over at her. She had a grim expression, too.

"This village is important to HQ. There's an imam there that hates the Taliban. Every village that fights the Taliban is one the U.S. wants to protect and help. So, we're going. Let's get this bird cranked up."

"You want me to fly right-hand seat?" Rachel wondered. She had been the AC, air commander, for the flight so far.

"No. You haven't been in that area and I have." Ty looked over at her. "You okay with that?"

"Yes, I am."

"Good, let's get the engines online and get that ramp up." He tried to keep the worry out of his tone. This wasn't a good thing and Ty knew it.

Rachel felt the tension in the cockpit. She looked at her watch. They'd scraped over the mountains and were heading down into a huge valley. Far ahead of them, she could see the Kabul River, a main water source through

Afghanistan. Farther south was Peshuwar, an Afghan outpost on the border with Pakistan. She'd never been in this area before. In August, the flat land on either side of the dark green river was lush with grass. The thunderstorms came and went regularly throughout the summer, dumping water on the desert areas. It was one of the few times places looked vibrant for a little while.

Hamilton hadn't said much at all. His mouth was tight, and she could tell he was worried. They flew at eight thousand feet, and from this vantage point, the area they were heading into appeared beautiful and peaceful. Rachel knew that was an illusion.

"This area is high Taliban traffic?"

"Yes," Hamilton muttered. "Peshuwar is thick with Taliban, spies and like Dodge City of the 1880s. A den of snakes."

"You've flown here before?"

"Yes, we've delivered food and medicine to the small village that's now being flooded out."

"I've never seen the Kabul River before today."

"It's a cold, murderous river," he warned her. "People drive their trucks through the sandy, shallow areas, and a wall of water suddenly rushes down out of the mountains and washes them away. A lot of Afghans drown. It's the thunderstorms in the mountains dumping five inches of water into a creek that flows into the river. There's a tidal wave and it comes out of nowhere. People can't see it coming until it's too late. And that water's hypothermic. It comes straight off glaciers. We routinely will get calls for flood rescue at least five or six times in the summer."

"I hope we get there in time," she said, worried.

"Me, too. Depends upon a lot of things."

Feeling for the trapped people, Rachel continued to

use the binoculars and scan for possible missiles that could be shot at them. They had no warning equipment on board. Chinooks were utterly vulnerable to attack, unlike the bristling Apache gunship.

Sitting up, she trained her binoculars on the river that was rapidly coming up. "If we can find them, that means you have to hover just above the truck so they can climb in through the belly door."

"Right. The people from that village know the routine."

"How do we know they aren't Taliban disguised as villagers?"

"We don't. But this village is right on the curve of the Kabul, and it's a fortress against Taliban. We've rescued people from there before. Their imam has a radio and he has contacted Bagram before in these situations."

"Must be a trustworthy imam," Rachel muttered.

"He is," Hamilton assured her. "Let's start descent."

"Roger."

Rachel tensed as the Chinook descended from its safer altitude toward the lower one. The closer they got, the more of a target they became.

"Do you see a white Toyota truck stuck on the sandbar in the river?" he demanded, guiding the bird down to three thousand feet.

"No...nothing..."

"Stay alert," he said. "It might have been swept off into the river and is gone. And no one will ever find it or them. That river is deep and swift."

"Roger..."

As the Chinook hit one thousand feet and began to fly over the river itself, Rachel felt fear. She always did at this altitude. They were sitting ducks.

Suddenly, she saw a flash from the slope of the mountain to her left.

"Hamilton!" she yelled, pointing.

Too late!

Rachel's eyes widened. It was a missile, aimed right at them!

"Chaff!" Hamilton roared, slamming the Chinook to the left and taking evasive action.

The bird groaned at the hard left turn. The engines screamed.

Rachel released the chaff, an aluminum countermeasure that would hopefully lead the missile to it and not the helo. Her heart surged into her throat. She saw the smoking trail of the missile. Oh, God...

It was the last thing she clearly remembered. As the Chinook was wrenched around, the missile ignored the chaff and struck the bird in the rear.

Fire erupted through the cargo hold. The helo wrenched upward, and Ty fought the controls. Screeching metal was torn out of the rear, the shrapnel flying forward. Hamilton felt a hot sensation in his left arm. His whole focus was on the helo suddenly shifting and falling. They were falling...right down into the river.

Rachel had no time to call for Mayday. The shrapnel from the explosion had sent a large, jagged piece of aluminum into the console. It instantly destroyed all their ability to communicate. Sucking in a breath, she grabbed the arms of her chair. The Chinook jerked and jumped. She heard the flailing of the rotors. Suddenly, the rear engine rotor flew apart, the long blades whirling and whipping past them like scimitars.

Choking, Rachel knew they were going to die. Smoke filled the cabin, black and thick. Hamilton was doing his best to try and make a soft landing into the water.

The Kabul River came up fast as the Chinook plummeted like a rock into the icy, furious green water. The rear of the destroyed helo struck the water first. Rachel let out a cry and was savagely jerked forward and then slammed back into the harness. Her neck snapped, and her helmet jammed into the seat for a second. The water rushed into the cargo hold.

Rachel instantly yanked off her harness, and Hamilton did the same. She pulled off her helmet and threw it behind her. Now, they had to egress this sinking helo or they would drown. Hamilton looked deathly pale, but she had no time to ask why. He'd released his harness, ridded himself of the helmet and had used his booted foot to break open the escape window. She did the same on her side. The glass shattered outward.

Within seconds, water flowed into the broken windows. It was cold and shocked Rachel as she took a huge breath. Somehow she wriggled and escaped out the window. Within seconds, she was swimming for her life. Cold water surged over her head as she flailed. The water was freezing. Her flight boots dragged her down. Striking out, Rachel kicked hard and finally broke the surface.

Gasping, water running into her eyes, she saw they were closer to the left bank of the river. Hamilton? Where was he? Unable to call him, she dodged another piece of the helo as it sank with ripping, tearing sounds, and then it gurgled beneath the foaming water. She didn't realize just how deep this river was until the Chinook completely disappeared from sight.

Rachel jerked her head around looking for Hamilton. And then…she saw him…floating, unconscious. *Oh,*

God! Without a thought for her own survival, Rachel swam straight toward his body. She grabbed his arm and managed to pull him so his head came out of the water. He was out cold. Sobbing, the current carrying them swiftly downstream, Rachel felt no confidence in their survival. In five minutes, hypothermia would set in. She'd become disoriented, her muscles would freeze up, and she would no longer be able to swim. God, no.

Chapter 9

Rachel swallowed a lot of water as she worked to bring her arm across Hamilton's chest. She went down, struggling to keep his head above water. The current was swift and icy cold. Flailing, she kicked hard, her boots tugging her downward. As she broke the surface, water exploded out of her mouth, and she gasped for air. Hamilton's head lolled against her shoulder and neck.

Adrenaline surged through her. Since they were closer to the left bank of the Kabul River, she struck out with her arm. Her efforts were impeded as she was suddenly hit from beneath the surface by a piece of the helicopter fuselage. The metal, unseen, twisted her around so that they were now looking upstream. Her eyes widened with terror. There, on the right bank, several lights flashed from the same hillside that had brought them down. The Taliban were firing at them!

Rachel gulped and allowed the current to carry them

swiftly downstream to escape the incoming artillery. The first explosion landed far above them, but the concussion blast made her ears hurt and ring. Kicking constantly, she kept them pointed toward the far shore that was thick with trees.

She heard the artillery scream and then it stopped. No! She tried to shield Hamilton with her body knowing it would land close. When the shell struck the dark green surface, it sent up a geyser twenty feet high, into the air. And when it exploded, an enormous wall of water threw Rachel and Ty ten feet farther down the river.

Rachel felt the blast pound against them. Much to her surprise, the tidal wave created by the blast beneath the water sent them closer to the bank. Choking, she continued to flail with one arm toward that shore. The river curved and they drifted around it. Rachel used the curve to actually get closer to the bank. Water kept striking her face. The cold was slowing her movements. She could no longer feel her body. Her feet felt like she had fifty-pound weights on each leg. Sobbing, Rachel knew she had to get out of the water or they were both going to sink and drown.

Within five feet of the shore, her boots struck bottom. With a cry of triumph, Rachel thrust forward, pulling Hamilton along. Her shoulder ached, and her arm had no sensation left. With each movement, she came out of the icy water. She sobbed for breath, her energy spent. She hooked her hands beneath Hamilton's armpits and dragged him out of the water and onto the shore.

Falling to her knees, she looked upstream. They had made the curve, and she knew that for the moment, they were unseen by the enemy. But that wouldn't last long.

Rachel wiped the water from her eyes with her shaking hands. There was thick brush and a grove of pine trees right in front of them. All she had to do was drag Hamilton into the area.

Looking at him, Rachel noticed a large, bloody gash on the left side of his skull. A piece of the torn Chinook had struck him and knocked him unconscious. Shakily, fear rising in her, Rachel pressed her fingers against his carotid artery at the left side of his bloody neck. She could feel a strong, solid pulse. He was alive! Just knowing that gave her the energy she needed.

If she didn't get them hidden shortly, the Taliban would find them. The enemy had radios, and even though they were on the other side of this river and unable to cross it, she knew they would call the closest Taliban unit on their side of the river. Gasping, she got to her feet. Dizziness swept over her. Staggering, Rachel shook her head. She had to think! She had to have the strength to get them to safety. They had to hide.

Groaning, Rachel gathered up his head and shoulders against her chest. She hooked her hands beneath his armpits and tugged hard. He was heavy. Grunting, she again jerked one more step backward. Every time she thrust using the heels of her boots digging into the sand, they made progress. It took a minute, but in the end, Rachel had them hidden in the thickets.

On the other side of the thickets was room to allow Hamilton to stretch out. Trembling violently from the cold and exertion, Rachel had to turn him over on his back since he probably had swallowed a lot of water. It needed to come out. Turning Hamilton so he was on his belly, she pulled his arms up above his head. She straddled his lower back, took her hands and pushed with all her might against the center of his back where his lungs were located.

A gush of water came out of his mouth. Heartened, Rachel continued to push against his torso. In five pushes, all the water was out of his lungs. It was then that he groaned.

Quickly getting off him, Rachel turned him over. She brought his arms down and knelt near his shoulder, anxiously watching his face. It had been deathly pale, but now, she could see pinkness coming back to his cheeks. When his eyes fluttered open, she sobbed.

"Ty? Ty? Are you all right? Can you hear me?" Rachel leaned over him, voice rasping. He tried to focus on her. At first, his blue eyes looked dull and murky.

Ty heard Rachel's hoarse, trembling voice. It felt like a drum reverberating inside his brain. Pain throbbed unremittingly on the left side of his head. As his vision began to clear, Hamilton belatedly realized that Rachel was leaning over him, an expression of terror on her face. Why was her hair wet and bedraggled around her shoulders? Her face was pale.

"Speak to me, Ty."

He opened his mouth. There was a brackish taste in it. He felt like he was drifting in and out of consciousness. Not only that, he was becoming aware of a deep ache in his upper, left arm. He began to shiver. Cold seeped into him. What had happened? When Rachel reached out, her hand brushing his cheek, he felt how cold her hand was. Frowning, he held her frightened gaze. What had happened?

"Talk, dammit!" Rachel whispered, inches from his face. Looking up, she quickly gazed around the area. Her ears were still ringing from the artillery explosions. She would never hear the Taliban sneaking up on them.

"Wh-what happened?" Ty rasped. He felt her hand leave his cheek. Instantly, he missed that connection with her.

As quickly as she could, Rachel said, "We got shot out of the sky by the Taliban. We crashed into the Kabul River. I just got us out, and we're now hiding in some bushes along the bank."

Suddenly, all of it came back to him. He lay there on the ground, staring up at Rachel. She was shaking, her uniform plastered against her body, her arms wrapped around herself. His own terror raced through him. When he tried to lift his left arm to touch his head, the pain was unbearable. With a grunt, he found he couldn't.

"Help me sit up," he told her.

Nodding, Rachel slid her arm beneath his neck and eased him up into a sitting position. Hamilton drew up his legs, and he placed his right hand on his brow. "You're hurt," she told him, her voice wobbly. "When the Chinook went down, you egressed out the window and into the water. A piece of the metal must have cut you and knocked you unconscious. I didn't see it happen." Rachel moved to Ty's left side so she could get a better look at the injury on his head. There was at least an inch-long gash that had laid his scalp open. It was bleeding heavily, the blood flowing down his neck, shoulder and soaking into his wet uniform.

"Where's the enemy?" Hamilton demanded, raising his head and trying to think through the haze of pain.

Rachel pointed across the river. "Over there and up on a hill, probably a mile away from us. The river carried us around a bend. We're out of sight for now." Rachel pushed the hair off her face and muttered, "I'm hoping they think they killed us with those two artillery rounds. That way, they won't start hunting for us."

"Good," he rasped. As he lifted his head, the pain almost blinded him. Biting back a groan, he asked, "Are you okay? Hurt?"

"No, I'm fine," Rachel whispered. She managed a twisted smile. "You were knocked unconscious. I didn't know that until you floated around the wreckage, and I caught sight of you." She reached out and touched his bloodied left hand. "I was so scared."

Ty moved his hand and cupped her cold, white fingers. "I don't remember anything," he said, his own voice sounding like gravel.

"You swallowed a lot of water." Rachel wanted connection with him right now. They were in enemy territory and they were alone.

Looking around, Hamilton tried to reorient. "We got hit. I remember that. The helo's rear lifted up."

"Yeah, that's where we took the hit," Rachel said. She studied the heavily bleeding head wound. Releasing his hand, she sat down and pulled the Velcro open on the deep, right-thigh pocket of her uniform. "We didn't have time to grab out egress bags," she told him.

Hamilton watched her dig around in the pocket. "What do you have in there?"

"A radio, dressings, antibiotic packs, needle, thread, aspirin," she muttered. Pulling it all out, she picked up the radio. It was wet. "I hope this works. We need to call for help."

Heartened, Ty said, "Make the call." Would it work even though it was waterlogged? His radio had been in his egress pack. Now, it was at the bottom of the Kabul River. Holding his breath, he watched as Rachel turned the small, round dial that would turn it on. When on, it would flash a small, green light on the front. Nothing happened.

"Oh, damn," Rachel muttered, twisting the dial again and again. "It's not working."

Hamilton heard the low edge of fear in her voice. "It's not designed to be dunked in water," he said, trying to make her feel better. He saw the desperation in her face, her mouth working as she turned it on and off several times. "Maybe it needs to dry out, and we can try it later?"

"We don't have later, Ty." Rachel had used his first name without even thinking about it. "We've got to get help. I know the Taliban will be looking for us."

No matter how many times she tried, the radio refused to work. Sitting there, the device in her hand, Rachel gave him a look of anxiety.

"Look, we need to take evasive action," he told her. "We didn't have time to make a Mayday call to Bravo. No one is going to miss us until we don't show up an hour from now."

"Did you call in our changed flight?" she asked.

"No, I thought you did."

Staring at him, Rachel realized it had been her duty to do that. And she'd failed. "Oh, God," she uttered. "I didn't. Bravo will think we're flying a straight line from Samarigam back to Camp Bravo." That one mistake could well cost their lives.

Hamilton felt grim. Shaking from the cold and trying to think through the blinding headache, he rasped, "There was a lot of distraction at the village."

Rachel had never expected him to say that. Blinking, she whispered, "I'm really sorry, Ty."

Hamilton gripped her hand, squeezed it once and released it. Right now, he felt raw, but he wanted to erase the fear he heard in her voice, the reality of their situation. "Let's concentrate on evasion. We need a plan. And where we're going."

Rachel knelt beside him. "We need to get this bleeding stopped." She tore open a packet. "Open your mouth, I'm giving you the antibiotics and some aspirin."

Hamilton nodded, tipped his head back, and she dropped a large, white pill into his mouth. It was hell trying to choke it down, but he did.

"I get to use all that first aid they taught us so long ago," she joked. Freezing, Rachel was grateful it was August, the temperature at seventy and it was sunny. If they were lucky, their uniforms would dry in a couple of hours. At nightfall, it dropped to the forties or even to freezing in this high mountain environment.

"Do what you have to do."

"That gash is long. I'm going to have to sew the edges together. God, I've never done anything like this before, Ty. But if I don't, it's going to keep on bleeding...."

Hearing the desperation in her voice, Ty murmured, "Take a deep breath, Rachel. It's going to be okay."

She spread out the items, steadied by his voice and the fact that he called her by her first name. He'd never done that before, but right now, she was grateful. Her hands stopped shaking so much. It was fear, she knew, but Hamilton's demeanor was one of quiet steadiness compared to how she felt inside. She marveled at his grace under pressure. "Okay, let me line up this stuff. Thank God I cram my flight pockets full of stuff."

"It's always a good habit to get into," Ty agreed. He closed his eyes. "Listen, can you do this when I'm lying down? I'm feeling dizzy."

"Sure, it will probably be easier." Rachel slid her hand beneath his neck and helped him lie down. "You're looking pale. What's going on?"

"Just exhausted," Hamilton admitted, closing his eyes. He'd nearly died, and he knew he was in shock.

Alarmed, Rachel realized she hadn't checked him from head to toe for any other injuries. "Ty, are you hurting anywhere else?"

"Yeah, my left, upper arm feels like it's on fire."

Scooting back, Rachel leaned down. She saw the arm of the garment had been slashed open. Pulling it back, she gasped. Another piece of shrapnel had cut deeply into his upper arm. "You've got another slash wound," she said.

"Bleeding bad?" he asked.

"No, not a lot. It's just very, very deep."

The concern in her husky voice flowed over him. He felt pretty light-headed. "Listen, do what you have to do. I'm feeling faint...."

Rachel watched as he lost consciousness. Stunned for a moment, she realized that there was no better time to sew up both wounds, because he wouldn't feel the pain. She grabbed a packet, ripped it open and applied the white powder of antibiotic across his scalp wound. She carefully folded up the packet and set it aside. The other half would go into his arm wound. Tearing open the next packet that said Lidocaine, she dripped part of it across his scalp. This medicine would numb the site so she could stitch it closed. Hands shaking, the hardest part was getting the thread through the needle.

Rachel was constantly dividing her attention between stitching up the two wounds and listening for enemy approach. Although they still wore their protective Kevlar vests, and each had a pistol strapped across their chest, it wasn't enough firepower against the Taliban.

The roar of the river hid other sounds. Rachel worked in silent terror as she did her best to bind Hamilton's wounds. She had used the small set of scissors to cut away some of the upper sleeve of his uniform to reach to the gash. To her relief, the scalp wound stopped bleeding once she'd stitched it closed. More than anything, Rachel was worried about infection setting in. If it did, he'd become feverish and unable to walk. And she knew they'd be doing a lot of walking very shortly.

It took an hour for her to finish. Hamilton's lashes fluttered a few times just as she got done wrapping his arm with a dressing and tying it off. When he looked toward her, she smiled.

"Welcome back to the world of the living. I just got done fixing you up. How do you feel?"

Closing his eyes, he whispered, "A little better."

"How's your head?"

Ty opened his eyes, turned his head and looked up at her. Her dark brown hair was drying around her beautiful face. Her gold eyes were dark with concealed fear. He managed a crooked, one-cornered smile of his own. "The pain has turned down ten notches. I almost feel human again, thanks."

"And your arm?" Rachel asked, relieved.

"I can't feel my hand," he said.

"Maybe that shrapnel sliced into a nerve?" she wondered. She saw him move his fingers.

"I don't know. Maybe it will go away in time," he uttered.

Sitting at his side, her hip near his left hand, she said, "An hour's gone by. I haven't heard or seen the Taliban yet."

Thirsty, Hamilton sat up with her help. As he scanned the area, he saw that she'd picked the perfect place to hide them. They were ringed with thick, tall bushes on the bank. "Did you hear a helo?" he asked.

"No..." Rachel said frowning.

Hamilton wiped his mouth. "I need to take stock of what I have. Let me dig into my flight pockets and find out."

Rachel got up and knelt nearby. "What are you thinking? Peshuwar is down farther on the other side of the river."

Ty pushed himself into a sitting position. He opened up both his Velcro flight pockets on his legs and placed his items beside Rachel's stash. "There's no way we can walk into Peshuwar. It's a den of thieves. The Taliban has a strong presence there. They see us in our uniforms, we're dead on the spot."

"You said there was an imam in Peshuwar who was pro-American. Maybe we could find him?"

"How?"

"I see your point."

Ty studied their cache. "Okay, we have ten protein bars between us. Antibiotics. Waterproof matches. A pair of scissors, a small penknife, one wet radio, two silver packs, which act as thermal blankets to keep our heat in, a compass and a map." Ty picked up the map. It had been coated, so it was waterproof. He opened it and spread it out between them.

"We're here," he said, putting his index finger down on the river, north of Peshuwar. Brow wrinkling, he squinted his eyes. "There's a very small village here, on the slope of the mountains we just flew over."

Rachel knelt, studied the area, and saw where he

was pointing. "That's a good fifteen miles inland, away from this river."

Ty looked up into her worried gaze. "There's a stream coming down off the mountains, through that village, and it flows right here into the river. We're going to need water."

"What's your ultimate goal here?" she asked.

"Survival," he said solemnly, "and reach Samarigam on the other side of that mountain range." He saw her eyes widen. "It's our only hope, Rachel. We're dead if we walk into Peshuwar asking for help. We know Samarigam is pro-American."

Nodding, she bit her lower lip and studied the map some more. "What kind of miles do we have to walk?"

"At least sixty miles, including the distance to this village on the map." Ty watched her face crumple. "Twenty miles a day. We can do it in three days. We'll have the brush and trees along that creek that leads up to this first village. We can travel in daylight."

"We'll never be able to travel at night in these mountains," she said. "And if we get to that village, there's no guarantee it isn't a Taliban stronghold, too."

"I don't think it is," Ty said, searching his memory. "The old CO of the last squadron told me that they'd flown in food and medicine to that village. Maybe they won't shoot us on sight."

Turning, Rachel straightened. She heard a dog barking across the river. She held up her hand. "Stay here. I'm going to see what or who is nearby."

Chapter 10

Rachel pulled her .45 pistol from the holster strapped across her Kevlar vest. Getting down on her belly, she moved through the thick brush to see about the barking dog. It sounded far away, as if on the other side of the wide, deep Kabul River. She prayed that was so and tucked her head down. She closed her eyes and pushed forward through the scratchy thickets.

Eventually, through the foliage from her hiding place, Rachel saw the dog. Her heart began a slow pound. There were five Taliban soldiers, all armed with AK-47s, standing on the other side of the river. A mangy, black mongrel dog, about fifty pounds, barked constantly. They were walking slowly along the other bank. Licking her lips, Rachel lay and followed them with her gaze. Were they the same group that had fired the artillery rounds at them? She didn't know. Her hand closed firmly over her .45.

It was obvious to her they were looking for something. Maybe signs of their footprints, showing that they survived the crash into the river? Eyes narrowing, Rachel watched as the group slowly moved upstream. They would bend down, look at the dirt and then straighten and move on. Yes, they were looking for signs they'd left the river and escaped.

She wriggled slowly backward through the thickets and finally got to the other side. She pushed up on her knees and looked toward Hamilton. He was sitting up, face pale, but alert. In his hand, he had his weapon, a .38. Getting up, she walked over and knelt at his side.

"There are five Taliban and a dog on the other side," she said in a low voice. "They were walking the bank of the river trying to find our tracks." Motioning toward the river, she added, "They just disappeared around the curve. Right now, we're safe."

Ty raised his brows even though it hurt. "They're going to try and make sure we're dead. The moment they know we survived, they'll bring every Taliban in the area down on our necks."

Rachel nodded, pushing the pistol back into the nylon holster across her chest. "Agreed." She gazed into his murky blue eyes. "How are you feeling?"

"The aspirin is taking hold," he told her in a roughened tone. "My head has finally stopped hurting so damn much."

"So," she teased, "you can think now?"

Just Rachel's partial smile lifted Ty's spirits. He managed a twisted grin back up at her. "Yeah, but we have a lot to think about."

Rachel sat down, drawing her knees up. "You're right, we can't go to Peshuwar. And it makes sense to follow that creek up to that tiny village on the top of the mountain. I just don't know if they will kill us or help us."

"Food and medicine has been dropped there before. We have to take a chance."

"I like the fact we can move up that stream under cover of the trees and bushes. We're less likely to be seen, and we can travel during daylight hours."

"This isn't going to be easy. When I move my head, I get dizzy. I don't even know if I can stand up and walk a straight line." Frustration settled in him over his condition. He was the helpless one. Rachel had survived the crash and was physically sound. He was not.

Reaching out, Rachel gripped his hand for a moment and gave it a squeeze. "I don't think help is coming to rescue us. Everyone at Ops will think we're on a beeline between Samarigam and Bravo. They'll be looking for us in the wrong area. And if you have to lean on me as we make it to that village, I don't mind."

The warmth of her fingers flooded his cold, chilled body. Ty continued to tremble from the cold flight suit against his goose-pimpled flesh. He saw the sincerity in her gold-and-brown eyes, and his heart opened. For one crazy moment, Hamilton wondered what it would be like to kiss Rachel. To feel the softness of her lips against his. Somehow, Ty knew she would be an incredible kisser. And then, shocked where his thoughts had gone, he sternly gave himself an internal shake. The crash must be making him think really stupid thoughts.

"If only your radio would dry out and work. That signal is set for the rescue channel on the radio at Ops...." Ty said.

"It's our only real hope," Rachel agreed, picking up the radio that she'd laid on a flat rock. "And it's only got so much battery left in it. I think we should keep it off and try it near sunset." Looking at her watch, she saw that it was 2:00 p.m. "I'm going to go reconnoiter the area. According to our map, that stream intersects the river about a quarter of a mile south of us. I want to make sure we can get there without being spotted."

"Good idea." Ty watched as she slowly rose and pulled out her .45. He managed a slight grin. "Why are you carrying that dinosaur of a pistol?" he wondered.

Looking down at him, Rachel said, "Because my father taught me if you want to stop a man in one shot, a .45 has the power to do it. I know the Army has other pistols that they prefer me to carry, but I want a big stick."

"Right now," Ty said, appreciating her logic, "that's exactly what is needed.

"Your .38 won't stop a man," she pointed out. "You'll have to fire three or four shots to stop him from charging toward you. That's a waste of bullets. We only have so many with us, and each one is going to count if we get into a firefight." Rachel pushed the drying hair off her brow. "One shot. One kill."

"Sniper speak," he said.

"My uncle Morgan was a sniper at one time when he was a Marine. When I graduated from flight school, he gave me this weapon as a gift." Rachel lifted the dull black pistol and gave it a fond look. "He knows his weapons. And carrying this pistol is like having him with me all the time. I love him very much...."

Hamilton could see it in the softened expression of her face and how her voice dropped and became suddenly husky with unseen tears. "Get going," he told her. "I'll stay here, lay down and try to rest."

"Good idea." She lifted her hand and said, "I'll be back as soon as I can...."

The pine trees were interspersed with leaf-bearing trees. Rachel walked silently in and around them. The good news was that the thickets ran almost solidly parallel to the bank of the green river. She would halt, hide behind a huge tree trunk and look around. Then Rachel would key her hearing to see if she picked up any sounds that meant a human being was near. When she could hear and see nothing, she would continue another hundred yards and do the same thing. It wouldn't get her to their objective fast, but she had no idea who or what inhabited this beautiful, green area.

Knowing that goat and sheep herders were everywhere and that they would use this river to water their herd, Rachel stayed especially watchful. Young boys were sent out to tend these herds. And she would not know if they were friend or foe. She didn't want to take a chance and remained guarded, her movements conservative. Overhead, puffy, white clouds came and went. To the north, in the mountain range, she could see dark, angry thunderclouds. Here on the flat of the valley, which was all desert except for the green ribbon of life on either side of the Kabul river, it appeared uninhabited. So far.

Rachel knew the Taliban was actively seeking proof of their death. They would be waiting for the bodies of two airmen to wash up on either side of the bank of this river. The Afghans were great trackers. As she moved silently down toward her objective, Rachel looked for brush on her way back and wiped out her tracks. There was no reason to think the Taliban wouldn't have men on this side of the river who were actively hunting for footprints right now.

Her heart never settled down as she held the gun up and ready as she walked. Every once in a while, as she stood with her back pressed to a trunk, Rachel would think about Hamilton. She'd saved his life, which struck her as ironic. He'd tried to end her career earlier in her life. And here she was saving his butt. Still, Rachel would have done the same thing all over again. Hamilton was a fellow aviator, U.S. Army and, therefore, a buddy. She would never have thought to let him drown when he was knocked unconscious.

Locating the stream, she knelt down by a pine tree and looked up. The creek was wider than she first thought. It was a good four feet wide and running strong with glacier water from high above. Rachel could see glimpses of the stream moving up the rocky slope toward the sharp peaks at least twenty miles away. Smiling a little, she closed her eyes for a moment. She opened them and slowly stood up. She broke off a pine branch and began to use it to destroy her tracks as she retraced her way back.

Ty never heard Rachel approach. He'd dragged himself over to a tree trunk and leaned against it, his weapon in hand. Startled when she seemed to appear out of nowhere, he saw her smile. Her dark hair framed her face. Her cheeks were red and it emphasized her large, intelligent gold eyes. Ty found himself wondering what the hell had possessed him to try and destroy her career. There was nothing but feminine strength and beauty, not to mention a powerful intellect, in Rachel. He began to appreciate what she brought to their collective table in this dire situation.

Rachel knelt near his left side. "How are you doing?" She had been gone a good hour. Hamilton's face had a bit of color to it now. He was no longer looking like a wan ghost.

"Better," he said. "What did you find?"

"We've got some luck on our side," Rachel said, smiling. She lifted her hand and pointed toward where the stream was located. "It's a lot wider than I thought it would be. Plenty of trees and brush to hide us for as far as I could see. I think if we get you up and walking, we'll be a lot safer." She looked up, her brows falling. "I know the Taliban has people walking the bank of this river on *our* side."

Ty nodded. "Yeah, and I'm jumpy as hell about it. It's only a matter of time before they'll be near our hiding place."

"Right." Rachel inspected his head wound. "It's stopped bleeding. Do you still have a headache?"

"It's gone," he murmured. "It's my arm."

Rachel examined the dressing she put around his upper arm. "It's a really deep gash, Ty. It's got to hurt like hell."

He shouldn't have liked the way his first name rolled from her lips, but he did. It sent an incredible, warm sensation through him. "It does. I've been trying to lift it, but I'm not doing too well. I'm just glad it was my left arm. I shoot with my right." He grimaced.

Rachel chuckled. "You need a sling for that arm. And I don't have anything to make it with." She looked around. "Maybe we'll find something along the creek."

"Don't worry about it," he said, tucking the .38 back into his chest holster. "Would you help me up?"

Rachel put her pistol away and walked around him. She held out her hand to him as he prepared to stand. "Hold on to me. I don't want you falling if you get dizzy."

Agreeing, Ty gripped her outstretched hand and was

surprised at her strength. He heaved himself to his feet. Instantly, dizziness struck him.

Rachel saw him start to fall. She stepped forward, slid her arm around his back and stabilized him. Hamilton had to lean heavily on her in order to stop from falling forward. "Easy," she whispered, keeping him in a tight embrace.

Ty didn't struggle. He was amazed she could take his full weight until he could regain his balance. She was incredibly strong. His arm had gone around her shoulders. She was five foot ten inches tall, two inches shorter than he was. Grateful that she anchored him, Ty fought the dizziness. Finally, it passed.

"Okay, I'm ready," he told her.

"Let's just walk together for a while," she counseled, glancing up at him. Rachel was once more aware of how incredibly good-looking Hamilton was. Truly, he could be the poster child on a U.S. Army ad for television. Definitely eye candy of the finest sort. And she found herself absorbing his strong body against her own, his arm around her shoulders. For a split second, Rachel wondered what it would be like to kiss him, to feel his body against hers.

Hamilton said, "Yeah, good idea. Until I know I can walk and the dizziness isn't going to nail us."

"Hold on…." Rachel leaned down and picked up her pine tree limb. "We're going to have to turn and cover our tracks as we go. Otherwise, the Taliban will find them and follow us."

Ty knew they would make a snail's pace toward their objective. "Let me try and do that." He held his hand out for the branch.

"Okay," Rachel said, keeping her arm firmly around him, her hand on his right hand. "Let's see if doing it causes you dizziness or not. If it does, I'll have to do it."

"I'll do it," Ty told her. Somehow, he had to be of help, and not utterly helpless.

"Okay, let's go…" Rachel urged in a whisper.

It was nearly 1600, 4:00 p.m., by the time they reached the fork that would lead them up the creek. Rachel saw the perspiration on Hamilton's furrowed brow. It cost him so much to continually turn, lean down and sweep their boot tracks out of the sand. Yet, he did it without complaining. His left arm didn't work well, but well enough to make the broad, sweeping movements. Rachel knew he was in a lot of pain.

"Let's sit down and rest," she counseled him. Guiding him to a thick pine tree trunk, Rachel helped him ease to the ground. She kneeled beside him. "Are you in pain?"

"Yeah, but that's all right," he muttered, feeling profoundly weakened. "I guess I'm not very good with a broom," Hamilton joked.

Smiling a little, Rachel peeked at the cut she'd made in his flight uniform arm. "Good, there's no blood showing on the dressing." She reached into her right thigh pocket and found some pain pills. "You need to take one. We've got a lot of hours of daylight left, and we've got to keep moving."

Ty didn't argue and swallowed the pill. He was thirsty. But to drink that water without purification tablets could be a disaster, too. Looking around, he spotted a plastic bottle near the stream. "Hey, go get that bottle, will you? We need something to put water in."

After spotting it, Rachel walked over and picked it

up. She laughed softly as she brought it over to him. "It's a water bottle! Just what we need."

"That village up above this creek received fresh water from the Army in their supplies. Some kid probably drank it and tossed the bottle into the creek. It eventually found its way down here."

"You're probably right." Standing, Rachel handed him the bottle and dug in her other thigh pocket. "I've got tablets that will clean the water."

"I made fun of you carrying an Army in your pockets, now I'm not," he told her with a slight grin.

"In the Apache we have an actual compartment with a bag that holds all this stuff," Rachel said. "When I found out I'd be flying Chinooks instead, I just transferred it all to my leg pockets. I'm glad I did."

"And I'll never make fun of your bulging leg pockets again," Ty swore. He saw her find a packet of water purification tablets. When he handed her the bottle, their fingers met and touched. Something good and warm flowed into Ty from that brief contact.

"I feel like a pharmacy on legs," Rachel gripped good-naturedly. "I'll be right back."

Rachel filled the quart-size bottle and dropped a tablet into it. She shook it until it dissolved. Walking back, she knelt down next to Ty and said, "Drink all you want." She handed it to him.

Ty guzzled about half of the cold, delicious water. "Here," he told her, wiping his mouth, "you take the rest."

Nodding, Rachel drank the other half of the water. Once more, she stood and refilled the bottle and put another tablet into it. "Ready to go?" she asked.

"Yeah," he muttered, pushing himself upright and using the trunk of the tree to stop him from falling.

Dizziness struck again. He closed his eyes, head resting against the solid wood. And then it passed.

"Okay?" she asked before tucking the filled bottle of water into her leg pocket.

Opening his eyes, he rasped, "Yeah. It wasn't as bad this time."

"Good. Ready?"

Ty said, "I am, but let me see if I can walk by myself."

Prepared, Rachel said, "Go for it."

"We'll make better time if I can," he panted. With an iron will engaged, Hamilton stepped away from the tree. The dizziness did not attack him. He grinned triumphantly over at her. "I can walk."

Rachel returned his grin. His blue eyes appeared less murky, especially with the pain pill taking hold. "Great." She picked up their pine broom. "You lead and I'll follow."

Feeling relief that he wasn't going to continue to be the helpless one, Ty gave her a thumbs-up sign. He pulled out his .38, and kept it in his right hand as he started slowly up the creek.

Rachel quickly covered their tracks and felt a bit happier and more relieved. She constantly looked around, her hearing keyed. They began to make good time up the gentle slope. They had survived a terrible crash. She was uninjured, and Hamilton was well enough to move on his own. Now, all they had to do was stay hidden, avoid the Taliban and make it to that tiny village on the side of the mountain.

Wiping her mouth, perspiration dotting her brow as she worked to erase their prints, Rachel realized something crucial. When night fell, they would be alone. And together. The sudden awareness of their intimacy panicked her. She had gone from hating Ty to liking him. He had been brave, courageous and a team player after the crash. She wiped her brow with the back of her sleeve. Now she understood as never before that Ty had changed. For the better. What was she going to do now?

Chapter 11

Ty fought with a vengeance the pounding headache that had come back. He attributed it to the ever steeper slope, which they quietly continued to navigate parallel to the creek. The trees would thin out here and there, and that was when they'd stop, look around, and ensure they wouldn't be seen before making it to a thicker grove of trees and brush.

Looking back, Rachel noticed Ty's face was becoming more pale. His mouth had tensed. When they got to a thick stand of pine and brush, she knelt down. He automatically knelt beside her.

"You're in pain?" she asked in a low voice.

Digging into his thigh pocket, Ty pulled out a packet of aspirin. "Yeah, it just came back. I'll pop these down and it should go away again."

"Let me check the wound," Rachel insisted. She got up and went to examine him more closely. One hand on Ty's shoulder, she gently moved his head a bit to get a good look at the wound. "It looks okay. There's no drainage. No sign of infection."

Absorbing her touch, Ty tried to keep things impersonal. "Good. It's just aftermath, is all. I'll be fine." How he wanted to reach out and grab her hand. This was all crazy, and Ty decided that the crash had made him emotionally vulnerable in a way he'd never been before.

"Here," she said, handing him their only water bottle.

"Thanks," he said, taking it from her.

"We've been climbing for forty minutes. A good hiking walk takes twenty minutes." She saw his Adam's apple bob several times as he downed the two tablets. His eyes were dull and she could tell he was in a lot of pain. Yet, he didn't complain. Rachel wasn't so sure she wouldn't have griped about it.

"We've probably gone a mile," Ty said, continuing to look around. The green strip that defined the creek quickly died and went back to the yellow grass and rocky soil. It was a barren, challenging landscape. "We're climbing and I'm slow," Ty added with a slight grimace.

"You're doing fine under the circumstances. How is your arm?"

"It would be nice to have a sling," he said. Holding it against his body kept it from really being painful. "If I drop my arm, it feels like it's on fire."

Rachel turned and craned her neck upward. "I don't see any village on that slope. Do you?"

Worry was evident in her tone. "It might be right on the creek, and we wouldn't see it from here," Ty said.

Rachel grunted. "You're probably right. Still,

we've got about two more miles to go, and it gets even steeper."

"That village is at seven thousand feet," Ty agreed. "I don't know if we should try to contact the elders in it or not."

"I know," Rachel said, worried. "They could be pro-Taliban."

"Most Afghan villages aren't," Ty said. He enjoyed simply looking at Rachel. She sat with her knees drawn up, arms around them. Her dark brown hair had dried and hung straight around her face. Cheeks red from exertion, she was a sight to behold. He wanted to kiss her. This time, he didn't overreact to the thought as he had before. Maybe because they were in a life-and-death situation, and the cards were stacked against them.

Glancing over at him, Rachel asked, "What do you want to do? Get close to it and hunker down for the night here at the creek? Contact them tomorrow morning?"

"No. It dives below freezing at night. All things being equal, I'd sure as hell like to be in a warm rock home with an elder than stuck out here."

"Mmm," Rachel agreed. Frowning, she muttered, "My ears are still ringing. I can't hear as well as I want to."

"It will go away within twenty-four hours," he said.

"I miss it. I'm afraid the Taliban will sneak up on us, and I won't hear them in time."

Reaching out, Ty briefly touched her hand. "Relax. My ears aren't ringing. We'll protect one another."

Warmth fled through her hand. Rachel was startled by his action. She could see Ty meant to give her solace. His fingers were long. *Flight hands.* Yes, he was a damn good pilot. Searching his eyes, she said, "Are you ready? Feel like going another mile?"

"Yeah," he muttered, getting to his feet. "Let's do it."

Rachel took the lead. She stayed as close to the bank of the gurgling creek as she could. The sun had moved to the other side of the peaks ahead of them, the mountains now in shadows on their side. The temperature had dropped. Rachel wished mightily for her thick, warm jacket but it had gone down in the Kabul River. Just moving kept her warm. Breath coming in gasps, she knew the altitude was getting to her.

By the time they'd gone another mile, Rachel called for a halt. Ty came and stood near her, his gaze fixed ahead.

"Do you hear that? Bells?" he asked.

"No," Rachel said. "Is that what you hear?"

"Yes," he said, focusing in on the sound. "I don't see anything but I know there's always a bell on the lead goat or sheep in a herd. Could be one nearby."

Mouth tightening, Rachel tried to see through the thick brush ahead but couldn't. "This would be a natural place for villagers to bring their livestock to eat and drink."

"Yes." Ty saw the worry in her features. "Since I can hear better than you, let me take the lead. You keep watch on our back."

Rachel nodded and moved aside. It was a good idea. Wishing she could hear better, she knew that her eyesight had to take over and make the difference. The creek had widened where they stood. As far as Rachel could see ahead around a slight curve, it continued to widen. It was perhaps ankle to knee deep here and there. Green moss floated along the bank. The grass, or what was left of it, was stubble. She was sure that the village's goats and sheep came through here regularly.

She pulled out her .45 and kept it in hand. Ty had pulled his .38. They had no idea who they might run into up above. Her heart was pounding from the relentless climb, but now, adrenaline started to flow into her bloodstream. Fear stalked her. Jittery, her nerves frayed by the near drowning after the crash, Rachel tried to focus.

As they rounded the curve of the creek, Ty suddenly went down on one knee, his pistol held up and ready.

Instantly, Rachel crouched behind him.

Ty made a signal with his hand and pointed to the other side of the creek.

Looking, Rachel saw a group of brown-and-white goats foraging up ahead. There was a young boy, about twelve years old, staff in hand, walking with them. The lead goat, a nanny with a leather collar and tinkling bell around her thin neck, took the small herd toward them. Rachel's heart began a slow pound. The boy wasn't armed and must have belonged to the unseen village above. She laid her hand on Ty's shoulder.

Twisting around, he looked at her.

"Let me get up and greet him. I know enough Pashto to speak to him. You stay hidden. If he runs or this is a trap, you can get away...."

Ty couldn't argue with her reasoning. He moved quietly into the nearby thickets, making sure he could draw a bead on the boy in case he had a hidden gun on him. Ty gave Rachel the signal to go ahead with her plan.

It was a risk but Rachel decided to put the pistol back in the holster across her Kevlar vest. If this boy was part of the unseen village, then he would know what an American helicopter pilot looked like. He'd be surprised to see her, a woman, but he would know she was American. *And, hopefully, a friend...*

The dark-haired boy was dressed in a long, blue vest, a white, long-sleeved shirt beneath it, brown trousers and, clearly, American, black hiking boots. Feeling a little more hopeful, Rachel eased from her hiding place. As she stepped to the bank of the stream, the nanny bleated and anchored.

The boy instantly looked up. His mouth dropped open.

"I come in peace," she called to the boy, giving him the customary greeting. "We need help. Can you take us to your elders?"

For a moment, the boy stared. Then his mouth clamped shut. He was frightened.

"Please," Rachel called to him in Pashto, "we are American. We need your help. Can you take us to your chief?"

Blinking, he called, "Where did you come from?"

"We were flying across your valley and we were shot down earlier today by the Taliban. We're trying to reach help."

The boy scratched his head. "Then it was *you!*"

Rachel didn't know what he was talking about. She did see the lad suddenly become excited. And then he raced to the other edge of the bank. "We saw your helicopter shot down earlier. My parents said the Americans died. But...you're here!"

Rachel smiled with some relief. "It's true. My friend, Captain Hamilton, is hurt. Can you lead us to your village? We need food and safety for the night."

"Of course, of course," the boy said. "I will bring my herd over. Wait!"

The boy sprang into action. In a blur, he quickly got

the twenty goats and herded them across the shallow stream. With his staff, he headed them up the slope. He then turned and stopped in front of her.

"I am Akmal!" He thrust his hand out to her, a big grin of welcome on his face.

Shaking his hand, Rachel said, "And I am Rachel." She turned and called to Ty, who emerged from the thickets.

Akmal became even more animated and officially introduced himself to the pilot. The boy seemed overjoyed to see them, his dark blue eyes glinting with excitement. When he noticed Ty's left arm, the bloody sleeve, he quickly took off a long cotton scarf from around his small neck.

"Here, Captain, use this to care for your arm."

Ty grinned and nodded.

Rachel took the scarf and fashioned it into a sling for his left arm. "We hit it lucky," she told him under her breath. "He's really glad to see us."

"Make that all of us," Ty murmured. His skin prickled where her fingers brushed his neck. "Thanks."

Rachel turned back to the boy. "I'd appreciate your taking us to your village. We need to talk with your chief."

"Of course," Akmal said. "Just follow me. Our leader is Hamid. He will be very surprised you lived. Allah has blessed you! Come!"

They set off at a fast pace. The goat herd trotted quickly up the mountain in front of them. Rachel walked behind Ty and kept watch on the rear. Both had put their pistols away as a show of peace. Within twenty minutes, the stone village came into view.

Rachel was amazed at how the rock homes blended into the yellow earth and rocky slope. The creek ran to the south of the village. She estimated there were twenty homes crowded together on a high bluff overlooking the valley and river below. She saw women in burkas, children playing and a couple of scrawny dogs. Though she wondered how they managed to survive in such an inhospitable land, her admiration for the Afghan people rose once more. They were tough and enduring, no question.

"Welcome to our humble village," the leader, Hamid, said to them.

Rachel and Ty sat with the gray-bearded elder in his rock home. Akmal had gone through the village proclaiming that the pilots were alive. Within moments, everyone had emptied out of their homes to stand in the street and greet them. To their relief, this village was clearly a safe place. Rachel had seen American clothing on all of the children. And each one wore shoes. In no time, they were shepherded to the end rock home where the elder of the village lived.

Rachel had been given a dark blue scarf to wear by one of the women before she entered the elder's home. "Thank you, my lord. We are so very grateful that you would take us into your home," she told Hamid. Indeed, it was warm, and finally, Rachel felt the tips of her fingers for the first time since the crash. Her uniform had dried, but she knew it wouldn't be enough against the frigid night air.

Semeen, the elder's wife, had her two daughters bring in plates of food for them. They handed each one a plate, bowed and then left.

Rachel thanked her, then noticed what was on the plates. It was American food—cheese, crackers and peanut butter.

Hamid said, "Please, eat. We know you are hungry."

Usually, their customs didn't allow this type of eating, but the leader obviously knew their plight. As Rachel and Ty dug in she asked the elder, "Do you have any way we can contact our people for help?"

Hamid shook his head grimly. "The only way to get help is to ride the trail down our mountain into the next valley and then get to the village of Samarigam."

Rachel knew there were no radios and cell phones out in this rough, wild country. "Would it be possible to send a horse and rider to that village to get us help?"

"No. The Taliban is hunting for you. They've already ridden through here twice. They've broken down the doors of my people's homes, looking for you."

Rachel interpreted for Ty. He immediately frowned.

"Will they be back?" he asked.

Rachel translated.

"No. They think that you probably died and drowned in the river," Hamid said. "But they wanted to make sure."

"I'm sorry this happened to you and your people," Rachel said to the old man. He was well into his sixties, his kind face deeply tanned and lined. There was a glint in his brown eyes that Rachel liked. He smiled often beneath his thick, long beard.

Hamid shrugged. "They know the Americans come here once a month. That is when they disappear. They know your Apache helicopters will destroy them. Once, there was an American Special Forces team here, but no longer. If they were here, they could call for help."

"I understand," Rachel said. Cheese and crackers had never tasted so good! She didn't realize just how starved she was until now. Semeen came back with warm goat's milk in cups for each of them and then quietly disappeared once more.

"I can keep you overnight," the leader told her. "You will stay with us. There is medicine for Captain Hamilton if you need it. The Americans keep us supplied and we are grateful."

Mind racing, Rachel said, "Do you have horses we can use?"

"I do. I have two very fine, part-Arabian geldings."

Rachel always kept a plastic bag that contained Afghan money. She pulled it out of her pocket. "I don't know how much they cost, but will this be enough?"

Hamid took the plastic bag, pulled out the thick wad of bills and counted them. He smiled. "More than enough," he said. "Thank you for paying for them."

Rachel knew that the money would go a long way toward making Hamid willing to help them. "You're more than welcome."

"If we get the horses," Ty said, "we need a disguise. We can't be seen riding in our flight suits or the Taliban will kill us."

Understanding his concern, Rachel asked the elder, "Is it possible that there is enough money there to buy two sets of clothing? I must appear to be a man. If the Taliban looks at us through binoculars and sees that I'm a woman, they'll attack us."

Hamid chuckled. "Indeed, they would, Captain. You will need a special turban that will not only hide who you are but allow a slit for only your eyes. That way, they will not be able to tell."

"I can handle that," Rachel promised him.

"Unfortunately, because the Taliban comes without warning, I'm going to have to take you to where we keep our herd of goats at night. There is a small room in there where you can hide." He frowned. "By Muslim law, a man and woman should not be together, but for your safety, this is best."

"I understand," Rachel murmured. "We're grateful you would help us." As she drank her warm goat's milk, her mind spun with shock. She'd be in a small room with Ty. They'd probably be sleeping together with a few blankets given by the villagers to keep them warm tonight. The sudden realization that she'd be in close quarters with him sent a frisson of fear through her. And on its heels, desire. Desire? Reeling, Rachel felt torn with indecision. That wasn't at all like her. Suddenly, her whole world had been upended.

Chapter 12

Rachel tried to keep disappointment out of her voice when Akmal showed them the small room off of the corral. The room was actually warmed by the thirty bleating goats. Most were bedded down for the night. Akmal pulled open the heavy wooden door with a leather strap.

"This will keep you safe in case the Taliban arrive at dawn. They hurt our people, steal our food and the grass we've pulled and dried for our goats to feed their horses." He wrinkled his nose in disgust.

Rachel put her hand on the young boy's thin shoulder. "This is fine. Will you come and wake us up tomorrow morning?"

"I will if the Taliban does not ride through," he promised. Moving into the narrow room, Akmal said, "Be sure to push the sacks and wooden boxes against the door. That way, if the Taliban comes in and pulls this door open, they will not realize you are hidden deeper inside the room."

Rachel shivered inwardly. "We will," she promised.

"Good night," Akmal said, lifting his hand.

The outer door to the barn closed. Rachel looked around. They had a small oil lamp that cast a very small amount of light, and she was grateful for the warmth. The smell wasn't bad because Akmal swept the floor clean every morning after the goats were let out to graze for the day.

Ty was already in the room, rummaging around, and she felt some of her terror receding. Hamid and his wife had fed them well, giving them both newfound strength. She walked into the room and set the lamp on a small shelf on the right wall.

"Need some help?" she asked.

Ty picked up a bunch of used gunnysacks that had UN painted on them. "Yes, you're going to have to get the crates out of here. I'm useless with my left arm in a sling."

She took the sacks from him and laid them near the door. "How are you feeling?"

"A helluva lot better," he told her. Straightening, Ty looked over his shoulder at her. Rachel's hair had been smashed by wearing the scarf. Still, her cheeks were rosy and her eyes sparkled. "Hot food in a safe place does wonders, doesn't it?"

"No question. We got lucky. Why don't you egress out of there, and I'll take care of those empty crates?"

Nodding, Ty backed out. With his left arm in a sling, the pain had stopped. Hot food had filled his growling belly, and the strength from eating it had been immediate. Rachel slid past him, her hips brushing against him. "I'll get the blankets and bring them in," he told her. His body tingled where she'd barely grazed him. The thought hadn't escaped Ty that they'd be lying very close to one another in a very narrow room. He pushed those feelings aside and forced himself to concentrate on getting the blankets and pillows that Semeen had given them.

In no time, their digs were in order. Rachel wiped the perspiration from her brow. "Come on in. I need you in here so I can build our wall."

Ty had brought the bedding in earlier. Stepping inside, he watched as she shut the door to the room and quickly built a wall with the empty wooden crates and grain sacks. They had been filled with food and other supplies from the United States. He knew all the crates, over time, would be broken down and used as firewood. Nothing was ever wasted out in this inhospitable area of the world. He got busy and spread the blankets across the dirt floor.

"There," Rachel said, pleased. "Does it look secure to you?" She picked up the oil lamp and brought it over to another wooden shelf jutting from the rock wall above where they would sleep.

Ty smiled. The woman had creatively used the fifty or so gunnysacks and hung them in such a way that no one could see through the wooden slats. There were two rows of crates to create a wall before anyone could get to them. "Good job," he praised.

He was sitting on the right side of their bed. Her heart beat a little harder in her chest as she went to sit by him. "This is really tight quarters," she muttered, uncomfortable.

"It is, but we'll make it work." Ty looked around. "The temperature is going to fall to near freezing." He picked up the two wool blankets that would be spread across them. "We're going to need these."

Ty had already taken off his Kevlar vest. His pistol was sitting on top of it, easy to reach. Rachel did the same. "God, it feels good to get out of this chicken plate," she griped. "I'll use it as a pillow."

"That stuff is so heavy," Ty agreed. "I'm leaving my boots on."

Rachel pushed her uncombed hair out of her face. "Yes. If something happens..."

"I think we'll be safe here tonight," Ty said, seeing the stress in her shadowed gold eyes.

Rachel didn't feel safe next to *him*. But she didn't say anything. He had taken his next set of pain pills, and he seemed relaxed but exhausted. He had more color to his face, and his blue eyes were clear. "I'm so tired," she uttered more to herself than him. Every movement took effort.

Ty laid down on his right side. He moved his injured left arm so that it was supported by his hip. "Makes two of us."

"I'm just glad Akmal has promised to stay up and watch for Taliban. I trust that if he hears them, he'll come and wake us up so we can escape before they arrive."

"The Taliban doesn't travel at night," Ty said. He watched Rachel lie down on her back. She then pulled the thick, wool blankets over them.

"Well, they do. Ask any Special Forces outpost over in Afghanistan, along the border," she muttered.

"Not on horseback, though. Remember, Hamid said the Taliban only ride in this area. They're not on foot."

Sitting up, Rachel picked up the oil lamp and blew out the flame. The room fell into a thick darkness. She carefully set it back on the shelf and lay down. The wool blankets were warm. "I know. But one thing we've learned about the Taliban is that they are creative, and you can't rely on them to do the same thing over and over again."

Closing his eyes, Ty was inches from her left shoulder. He inhaled the perfume that was only Rachel. The pillow kept his head raised, and he no longer had a headache. He hungrily absorbed the warmth radiating from her body. Not because Rachel was warm, but because he was powerfully drawn to her. When had the past disappeared and the present taken over? Ty didn't know. Like a thief and a beggar, he slowly inhaled her scent. It was like sucking life back into his numbed body. Rachel *was* life, he decided.

"You know," Ty began in a quiet tone, "you're an incredible woman."

The reverberation of his voice flowed through Rachel. She kept her eyes closed because she was exhausted. Yet, she felt wired. Her mind was wide awake. Her body was begging for sleep and rest. "Thanks," she murmured. It was a far cry from him trying to embarrass her in front of the other students at flight school. What had changed? Had they both grown up? Matured beyond their torment-filled pasts? Rachel hoped so, because she had no energy to continue to hold Ty Hamilton at bay. Their lives were on the line every second now.

Ty slowly rolled over on his back. "I can't sleep," he said, unhappy.

"Me neither. It's adrenaline."

"Yeah. Damn."

Smiling tiredly, the darkness so complete Rachel

couldn't see her hand an inch from her face, she said, "I feel safe here, though."

"Yes, so do I...."

Their voices were soft, so the sound didn't carry. Rachel could hear the bleat of a goat every now and then, but it sounded very far away. "I'm glad the walls are four-feet-thick rock."

"Makes two of us."

Her hand was touching his. With Ty on his back, there was no way to avoid contact. Rachel soaked up Ty's nearness. Heat rolled off his body, and she was comfortably warm. Even though the winds were blowing outside at this altitude, the rock barn kept them at bay.

"I remember when we were kids growing up that we'd take cardboard boxes and string my mom's sheets across them and make a house. My sisters and I played house for hours like that. This place kind of reminds me of that."

Ty heard the wistful tone in her voice and realized just how much he liked finding out more about her. "After my mom died," he said "play wasn't something my father had in mind for me."

"I think it's hard to be an only child," Rachel said.

"To hear my father tell it, children were good for only one thing—work."

Alarmed, Rachel said, "What?"

"It's a long story," Ty said. Yet, he felt the urge to tell her. Somehow, he knew Rachel would understand. "My father saw two things in me—football captain and worker bee."

"That's ridiculous!" Rachel said, frowning.

"I didn't mind. It kept me busy. It kept my mind off losing my mom as I grew up."

Her heart squeezed with compassion. "Do you remember your mother?"

"Vaguely," he said, closing his eyes. "I have a few photos of her. My father wasn't big on taking pictures. He said it cost money to get the pictures put on paper."

"I'm so sorry he was cruel to you," Rachel said, her mind spinning.

Ty turned his face toward her, his voice thick with regret. "I'm the one who owes you one hell of an apology, Rachel. You aren't weak. You've been the strong one here."

Rachel felt like someone had struck her in the chest with a hammer. All through flight school, he parroted the very opposite to her on a daily basis. He screamed hateful words in her face. She had to stand at attention and take it without responding. All it did was make Rachel more determined to win her wings. "No woman is weak," she said with emotion.

With a sigh, Ty whispered, "You're right...." He was remembering how he treated Rachel in flight school. Guilt washed through him.

"What changed your mind about us?" Rachel asked.

"I had five years to see women differently," Ty muttered. "After I was booted out of flight school, I was assigned to a Chinook squadron that had women and men pilots. Over time, I saw the women were just as good, sometimes better, than a man at the controls. My father was so filled with grief over the loss that he was taking it out on me."

"I remember. You were his whipping post," Rachel said, sadness in her tone. She itched to reach out and curve her hand around Ty's. She stopped herself. There was still a lot of pain from their past, so Rachel couldn't bring herself to do that.

"Yes, I guess I was. My father was lost without my mother. I realize that now. I didn't then."

"Well." Rachel snorted. "You were a child who had lost his mother, too. I would think your father had enough maturity to realize that."

"No, that didn't happen," Ty admitted. He rested his arm across his closed eyes. So many images and a gamut of feelings flowed from that time in his life. Somehow, just talking to Rachel soothed his injured heart.

"I still can't believe he wouldn't comfort you," Rachel said, disbelief in her voice. "Didn't he know you had to grieve? To cry for the loss of your mom?"

"When I cried, he'd whip me with a belt. He'd tell me to stop crying. Eventually, I choked down my grief. He hired a housekeeper by the name of Charleen Turner, who took over the cooking, cleaning and taking care of me."

Rachel sucked in a soft breath of air. "Were you able to bond with the housekeeper?" She tried to put herself in Ty's place. Knowing how much she loved her mother, she just couldn't imagine the psychic and physical damage done to Ty. No wonder he had hated women. But Rachel cautioned herself. Ty's father had beat him until he stopped his grieving for his mother. Then he'd been brainwashed by his angry father who couldn't rise above his own sorrow to help his baby son cope with the devastating loss.

"No. Charleen didn't like kids." He managed a croak of a laugh. "She was an alcoholic. My father knew it but didn't care. She was the only woman he could find who would come and live at the ranch. When she was drunk, I knew to hide and be seen, not heard. If I got underfoot, she'd complain to my father and he'd come in and beat me with a strap."

"My God," Rachel whispered in disbelief. "It's a wonder you survived. Didn't someone turn your father in for abusing you?"

"Who could?" he asked. "I lived thirty miles south of Cheyenne. Our closest neighbor was fifteen miles away, and my father never made friends. He's a bastard to this day. He's got a lot of people who fear and dislike him."

"But," Rachel sputtered, "surely your school teachers saw you were abused."

"No. My father made sure the strappings were on my back, butt and legs. No one ever knew...."

"Couldn't you have asked for help?"

"I tried to run away once when I was twelve. When my father caught up with me, he beat me within an inch of my life. He warned me to never tell anyone about the beatings. If I did, he said he'd disown me."

Rolling her eyes, Rachel growled, "Hell, you'd have been much better off with any family but him."

"I didn't know that, Rachel." Ty liked saying her name. It rolled off his lips like honey. "I was raised in a climate of fear. I wasn't about to say anything to anyone. I didn't know there was help out there." And then his voice lowered. "Look, I'd already lost my mom. I couldn't bear to lose my father, too."

In that moment, her heart broke for Ty. Rachel heard the little-boy fear in his voice even though Ty was now a grown man. "Our childhood can either support us or tear us apart," she agreed softly. She found herself wanting badly to hold him against the terrible pain he carried deep within himself.

"It took me a long time to understand what had happened," Ty said.

"Do you ever go home for a visit?" She couldn't think that anyone in their right mind would be around an abusive son of a bitch like that.

"Not anymore," Ty said, sadness evident. He took a deep breath, his heart beating hard with fear. He forced the words out. "Listen, Rachel, I need to apologize for the way I treated you back in flight school." His voice deepened with feeling. "I can't undo the past. You were right and I was wrong. You don't know how many times I picked up the phone to contact you and tell you I was sorry." His mouth thinned. "It took me three years in that Chinook squadron to come around and realize my father didn't do me any favors. I couldn't change him. What I did do is change myself, my attitudes toward women and try to rectify what I did wrong back then."

Rachel lay there, feeling his sincere words drain away her dislike of him. She reeled with all the information about his youth, his abusive father and an alcoholic housekeeper who doubled as his mother. Tears came to her eyes. She cleared her throat. "Thank you for telling me that. It helps."

Ty wanted to turn over and slide his arm beneath her neck, draw Rachel to him and simply hold her. Cautioning himself, he knew it would be too much, too soon. "I didn't have the guts to make that call," he warned her. "I was too afraid."

"I think I understand why," Rachel murmured. "Given your past, it makes sense now."

Swallowing hard, Ty wished mightily that there was light in the room. He desperately wanted to look into Rachel's eyes. To see if she really meant it. "I wanted to tell you, because if we don't get out of this fix alive, I at least want to be square with you."

Rachel fought back her tears. He was right: the chances of them getting out of this fix alive were very low. "I appreciate that."

Her soft, halting words were laced with tears. He could hear it in her husky voice. Closing his eyes, he clenched his teeth. He couldn't cry. He just couldn't. Finally, after several moments of pregnant silence, Ty rasped, "Thank you. You have no idea how good that makes me feel. I was hell on you at flight school. I didn't know it then, but I was doing the same thing my father did to me. You were a whipping post for all my grief." And then Ty did something so bold that it even surprised even him. He slid his hand beneath the blanket, sought and found Rachel's. Giving her hand a warm, firm squeeze, he added unsteadily, "Your forgiveness means everything to me, Rachel. Thank you for your courage...." He released her fingers.

Rachel was shocked by his hand around hers and felt tears flowing silently down the sides of her face. Quickly, she wiped them away. Ty's hand was not only warm but gave her a sense of security in a very insecure world. The sincerity of his voice shook loose so much old anger and hurt from those days. Rachel could literally feel the rage dissolving in her heart and flowing out of her like an unchecked flood. Relief began to fill her instead. She tried to think what to say, the right words. She wanted to cry for all the pain he'd carried for so long, unable to give it voice, to sob out his loss for his mother. His young, innocent love had been destroyed. Ty knew no other way. Until life had helped to reshape and change him. Other women had been role models to show him that women were not only strong, but intelligent. And they deserved to be in the military, flying a helicopter right alongside him.

When Ty heard nothing further from her, he added in a pained tone, "I know I don't deserve your forgiveness, and I'm okay with it, Rachel. I just…needed to get this off my chest and try to make amends before something happens."

Because she didn't trust herself, Rachel turned on her right side, facing the wall, her hands pressed against her face. The sobs tore out of her whether she wanted them to or not. And she didn't dare let Ty know that she was crying for him.

Chapter 13

"Are you ready?" Ty had just mounted his gray, part-Arab gelding that Hamid had given them. He was dressed like an Afghan soldier.

"Yes." Rachel had mounted her bay Arab gelding. Around her, the village had gathered in the dawn light to see them off. Akmal had come and awakened them an hour earlier. Despite last night's wrenching admissions from Ty, she had finally fallen into a deep, healing sleep. "Yes, I am," she said. Scared but ready. Smiling down at Hamid and his wife, who had their brown wool cloaks pulled tightly around them, she lifted her hand in farewell to them.

"If we make it to Samarigam, we'll see that you are paid for the saddles and bridles, my lord." They had only five horses total in the village, and Rachel knew they relied heavily on each of them for transportation.

"And we'll see what can be done about airlifting these two animals back to you."

Hamid nodded. "Allah be with you, Captain. It's a long, dangerous road."

"Thank you," she said. Turning her bay around, Rachel pulled the brown cloth across the lower half of her face. She wore a turban of the same color, a dark green, wool cloak over her shoulders. It felt good in the freezing morning air.

Everyone waved as they left the village and rode down the prominent trail. The sky was dark above them, stars faint along the eastern horizon. The breath of the horses as they plodded steadily down the winding, twisting path, resembled jets of steam coming out of their nostrils. There was enough room for them to ride side by side. Rachel pulled abreast of Ty. He was dressed in a brown turban, the cloth hiding his lower jaw. If the Taliban saw him without a beard, they would know he was a foreigner. Her leg brushed occasionally against his as they rode.

"Beautiful, isn't it?" she asked in a quiet tone.

Looking around, Ty kept searching for possible Taliban on this well-used trail. "If you call freezing your butt off this morning, I guess." He grinned over at her. All he could see were Rachel's eyes. The rest of her clothing, which was male, covered up the fact she was a woman. The rifle she carried was slung across her back.

Chuckling, Rachel nodded. "It's pretty cold." How badly she wanted to talk with Ty, but they had to remain alert. Hamid had warned them that this trail was used by Taliban and merchants going between the villages. He had made sure they were dressed to look like they came from his village. Each one had distinctive costumes and colors. Earlier, Akmal had put red tassels on the bridle of each horse. That would identify them as being from the village, as well. If the Taliban saw them, then there was less chance of being stopped and questioned by them.

As Ty continued to look around, the steep slope of the mountain and the rocks on the trail made the horse pick its way carefully around the objects. Overhead, the sky was beginning to lighten. Everything was silent except for an inconstant breeze that would wind through the yellow, rocky mountains surrounding them. He was glad that Hamid had loaned them two rifles with a box of ammunition. It wasn't much protection, but it was better than what little they had. He was fearful of meeting a group of Taliban on the trail but kept his thoughts to himself.

"I tried that radio again this morning," Rachel told him. "It still isn't working."

"Our luck. We're going to have to make it to Samarigam."

Nodding, Rachel enjoyed the sway of the horse between her legs. The animals were small, tough and hardy. "How far to the well? Hamid said we should reach it midday?" Fondly patting the horse on its shaggy neck, Rachel knew they would need water to keep on going. Luckily, Hamid said there were two wells on the trail. It was forty-five miles between the two villages. They couldn't trot or run their horses down the steep switchback trail. If a horse stumbled and fell, it could break a leg as well as injure the rider. This would take more time than Rachel had anticipated. She tried to quell her frustration.

"Hamid said ten miles to the first well. He said we'd

drop into the valley over there." Ty pointed to two steep mountain passes they had to ride through.

Rachel grimaced. "I don't know how these horses are going to go that far without water."

"They will," he said. "It won't be easy on them, but they've made this trip before."

"They're tougher than we are, that's for sure," Rachel said, patting her gelding again.

The trail straightened out for a bit as it headed down the rocky mountain. Ty looked over at her. "I'm glad we had that talk last night. I didn't know I'd be doing the talking, though." He searched Rachel's warm, gold eyes. "I apologized to you last night, but I wanted to do it this morning, too. You deserved to be told to your face." His heart beat a little harder in his chest, and it wasn't from the altitude. He wished that he could see Rachel's face right now.

Rachel swallowed hard. "I accept your apology, Ty. Honestly, I never expected one from you."

"When I found out you were assigned to me, I knew I had to do it." Ty managed a half smile. "It was a long time in coming. Frankly, I never thought I'd see you again."

"That makes two of us," Rachel said, chuckling. "When I found out I was assigned to your squadron, I was not a happy camper."

"I don't blame you for feeling like that."

Searching his eyes, Rachel said, "You grew up in those five years."

"Yes, I did. I never thought I'd get a chance to tell you that I was sorry for what I did to you."

Sadness moved through her. She wanted to reach out and touch his arm, but she didn't dare. Someone could be watching them, hidden in the rocks and huge boulders, which were everywhere. "I felt so bad for you, Ty. I didn't know you'd lost your mother. And your father didn't treat you right."

"I survived."

"I can't conceive of losing either of my parents," she whispered, brows dropping. "I tried to put myself in your place last night, and I couldn't go there. I rely on them so much. Even to this day, I do."

"You're lucky," Ty told her. He saw her eyes were fraught with sadness. For him. For whatever reason, it felt good to have Rachel think well of him for once. He'd done so much damage to her and had tried to obliterate her career, yet she'd forgiven him. Ty's heart swelled with inexplicable joy over that realization.

"I am. But I worry now. I'm sure the Army has contacted my family and told them I'm missing in action. My mom is probably crying. My dad, I'm sure, has contacted Uncle Morgan to see what he can do to find me."

"I'm sure my father could care less," Ty muttered.

"That's really sad."

"We split five years ago. I haven't been in contact with him since that day."

The pain was clear in his voice. Rachel saw it in his narrowing eyes, which became dark with obvious grief. "The Army will tell him, though."

"I know." Ty gazed up at the sky. The stars had disappeared, and in their place, a dark blue color remained. "I don't really care."

Rachel didn't believe him, but what could she say or do? *Nothing.* Compressing her lips, she said, "It's hard on everyone when we turn up missing."

Something made him ask, "Do you have a significant other?" He hoped not, but there was no way Rachel wouldn't be involved. She was too beautiful, poised and intelligent.

"No, thank goodness, I don't." Rachel looked over at him. "What about you?"

"No one," he said.

"You're not married? Have kids?"

Hearing the teasing in her voice, he smiled a little. "No, I haven't been very good in the relationship department. It's taken me five years and a lot of hard knocks with women to get straight about what makes a relationship run or not."

"You were sorting out your father's view on life from your own?" Rachel guessed. Why did she feel a soaring happiness when Ty said he wasn't involved with another woman? She secretly guessed that his hatred of women would cause all kinds of hell in a relationship. And until he got rid of that perspective, no woman worth her salt would put up with Ty's antics or behavior.

"Yes," he said. "I began seeing the way he treated my mother. Not that I remember much, but he was always yelling at her. Even as a young kid, I knew that was wrong."

Rachel shook her head. "He was a parent out of control. You don't yell at someone you love. You try to work it out."

"It sounds as if you know something about a good relationship," Ty said.

Pain moved through her heart. "Okay, confession time," she told him.

"Your secrets are safe with me."

Rachel smiled. "A year ago, I was engaged to be married. I met Garrett in Afghanistan. He flew with an Apache squadron out of Helmand Province."

Ty could tell by the roughness in her voice that something had happened. He remained silent.

"There was an attack on his base and he was killed," she finally admitted. Giving Ty a quick glance, she saw the worry in his exposed face. "I loved him so much. We were the best of friends."

He had to stop himself from reaching over to touch the hand that rested on the saddle. "I'm sorry. I really am. He had to be one hell of a man to get your attention."

"He was." Rachel closed her eyes for a brief moment. "Sometimes, it seems like it was just yesterday. On other days, it seems years ago, as if it was a dream, not reality."

"I remember when my mother died, I had days like that, even at three years old."

Her heart broke for Ty. She gazed over at him and thought he was as lost in the past as she was. "My parents always told me that life wasn't easy. It consisted of ups and downs. As a kid it was a concept, not a reality."

"And being here, we lose people nearly every day," Ty agreed. "Good friends..."

"Yes," she said. "This last year has made me realize I have to grab life and live. I can't think about a future. I have to be here. Now," she said, pointing her index finger at the ground.

"I've learned to hide," he admitted. "No love life."

Giving him a confused look, Rachel asked, "What do you mean by that?" Ty Hamilton was a brazen, courageous pilot. He was a man who dripped with leadership and intelligence.

"My track record with women is bad. Each one took a little bit more of my father's attitude out of me. But it was wearing on them, too. For the last year, I've been without a relationship. I didn't want another bruising round with another woman. I kept hoping for a good connection, but it never happened." *Until now,* a voice whispered to him. Ty shook his head. "I'm not exactly the type of man any woman is looking for."

Rachel disagreed but said nothing. "We're all in the learning mode, Ty. And we all make mistakes. All the time."

"Yeah," he sighed, "but not mistakes you could drive a Mack truck through." He managed a derisive laugh.

Knowing he'd been through a rough five years and was trying to turn himself around, Rachel said, "In my eyes, you're making good changes, Ty. Getting rid of your father's crap and then trying to discover who you are instead takes time."

"It's been five years," he said, smiling. "That's a lot longer than I ever wanted it to take."

Laughing, Rachel understood. As they crested the trail, they halted their horses. The next mountain looked even steeper. "If you think you're done changing, you have another think coming. My mom always said that we're a work in progress. The shaping, carving and trimming are never finished."

Ty sat up in the saddle to give his sore rear a break. He couldn't see anyone on the trail. Breathing a sigh of relief, he turned to Rachel. "A work in progress? That definitely fits me. Ready for the next mountain?"

"Let's go." She looked at her watch. "We're making good time."

"It's the company," Ty called over his shoulder as he guided his horse down the trail.

Rachel couldn't disagree. The trail was wide but not wide enough for the horses to walk side by side. "It is," she said, smiling. Just getting to talk with Ty made her feel hopeful. He'd come a long way. Her heart expanded with a quiet joy. Funny, she'd never felt like this about any other man. Not even Garrett, her fiancé. What was going on between them? Rachel didn't know, and she couldn't afford to dwell on it right now. Leaning over, she patted her horse. "I don't know about you, but I'm looking forward to that first well. My butt is killing me!"

Rachel groaned as she stepped onto the grassy area of the well, ancient and made of rock. A few scraggly trees grew around it. She had handed the reins to Ty. There was a bucket and crank. After pushing the wooden pail over the opening, she quickly lowered it. There was a splash at about twenty feet. Once she quickly wrenched the pail up with the wooden handle, they had water. The horses nickered and crowded closer. For the next ten minutes, she filled pails of water for the thirsty animals.

Ty studied the area. They'd come off the last slope, and the well sat about a mile from the actual valley between the mountains. The green looked out of place compared to the yellow, rocky dirt that surrounded them. It was 1:00 p.m., the sky a light blue with puffy white clouds dotted against it. The temperature had risen, and he was actually hot in the wool clothing.

"We're next," Rachel called, hefting the bucket down on the ground near his feet. Hamid had given them a small wooden cup, and she pulled it out of the saddlebag her horse carried. Dipping it into the water, she straightened and handed it to Ty.

"Thanks," he said before swallowing deeply.

While he was drinking water, Rachel retrieved the empty plastic bottles to refill them. The wind was inconstant, and she longed to pull the hot fabric away from her face. It was much warmer in the valley. She ached for a cool shower.

"Your turn," Ty said, handing her a mug filled with water.

Smiling, she put the bottles down by the well and accepted the welcome gift. "Thanks."

The birds were singing in the scrawny nearby trees. Far above, Ty thought he saw an eagle floating on the unseen air currents. There was nothing but natural sound. The horses were eagerly nibbling at any piece of green grass they could find. They had to be hungry. Looking back, he allowed himself the pleasure of watching Rachel drink. She was beautiful. An ache began in his lower body, but he quickly shoved the desire away. While it was true there was a white flag of surrender symbolically held between them, he didn't think she'd be interested in him as a man. Not after what he'd done to her. Sadness swept through him, and he took the horses over to a thick patch of grass.

After she finished filling the water bottles, Rachel put half of them in the saddle bags of Ty's horse and half in her own. Rubbing her wet hands on her trousers, she went over to where he was standing. The horses were famished. Hamid had advised them to let them eat for half an hour before moving on across the valley. She put a hand to her eyes, looking at the steep mountains on the other side.

"That's a lot of hard climbing ahead for us and the horses," she said.

"It is. Beautiful valley, though," he said. "A few days ago, we flew right over this area and didn't give it a second look."

Rachel chuckled. "Things change."

Didn't they? Ty forced himself to stop looking at her. Her male clothing couldn't hide those glistening gold eyes of hers. Again, he wondered what it would be like to kiss her. Would she allow him to do that? Ty didn't think so. But damn, he wanted to kiss her. Their talk last night had sprung open an old door that had been blocked deep down inside. She had released something primal within him. He tried to name it. Was it her nurturing personality? God knew, Ty wanted to be held in her arms. Somehow, she fed his thirsty, starving soul. Fed his heart that ached to be loved fully by someone. For so long, Ty had been without real love. Acknowledging that he was at fault in his past relationships, he knew he had to continue to make changes so that a woman would want him in her life.

"Ready?" Rachel asked. She saw him grow pensive. The energy around Ty shifted. He was completely immersed in his thoughts. When he lifted his head and met her gaze, he nodded.

"My butt is numb."

"So is mine," she laughed. Rachel took the reins of her horse from Ty. Mounting up, she appreciated Ty's struggle to get back on the horse. His left arm was in a sling. Yet, he made it. There was determination in every bit of his face. "How's the pain?" she wondered.

"Manageable," Ty said, picking up the reins. "I just took another pain pill."

"Good." Rachel joined him as they walked their horses together down the widening path. It felt good to be on flat land. There were trees here and there, casting shade across the grass. Looking around, she said, "I'm surprised we don't see any goat or sheep herds down here."

"Me, too." Frowning, Ty muttered, "I wonder if that

means the Taliban is around. I know villages keep their herds protected when they're in their area. The Taliban eat the animals."

"Bastards," Rachel gritted out. "Every sheep and goat is important to the people of these villages."

"It's their way of telling the villagers they're in control."

Snorting, Rachel agreed. Ty kicked his horse into a slow trot and so did she. It was ten miles across this narrow valley bracketed by steep, nine thousand foot high peaks. She noticed on the other side of the valley there were a lot of caves. This was a favorite hiding place for the Taliban. Yet, she saw no shapes or horses to suggest the enemy was nearby.

Suddenly, Rachel heard a noise behind them. To her shock, she saw at least ten horsemen coming at them at a fast gallop.

"Ty!"

Rachel's cry made him turn. His eyes widened. There, about five miles away, was a group of horsemen coming at high speed. And there was no way to tell if they were friendly or Taliban. He'd seen several small canyons near the end of the valley. "Follow me!" he yelled and clapped his heels to his horse.

Instantly, Rachel followed at a fast gallop, so fast that her eyes watered. The pounding of the horse's hooves dulled her hearing. Ty led her into the canyons at the end of the valley. Turning in her saddle, Rachel saw their weapons. And they were firing at them!

"Enemy!" she shouted.

Ty nodded. He whipped his horse and chose the center of three canyons. They were steep and filled with brush and trees. The horse grunted and leaped over some fallen logs as it scrambled high into the canyon.

Jerking a look around, he saw Rachel was right behind him. For the moment, they had made a turn and were out of sight of the enemy. Urging his mount up into the tree line, Hamilton prayed the horse wouldn't fall on the rocky ground. They had to be hidden! Breathing hard, he guided his brave horse higher and higher. Was this a box canyon? Or did it spill out onto the slopes above it? Ty didn't know. If it was a box canyon, it could mean their death. *Oh, God, let me have made the right decision....*

Winded and frightened, Rachel dismounted as Ty had. They were very high up in the canyon. They were at least a thousand feet off the valley floor. Gasping, she quickly brought her horse up beside his.

"Definitely Taliban."

Wiping his mouth after he pulled the fabric away, Ty peered down the canyon. "They can't see us up here."

"There are three canyons," Rachel breathlessly agreed. "I wonder if they'll hunt for us?"

"I'm counting on it," he growled. Looking around, he said, "I'll be damned. Look.... A cave!"

Turning and following where he was pointing, Rachel saw a sliver of an opening to a cave. It was hidden by thick brush. "Let's get in there."

"Right," Ty agreed. Leading his horse, he clambered up though the rubble another five hundred feet before reaching the opening. Without waiting, Ty plunged into the slit in the wall of the rock.

Rachel followed. They halted inside and looked around. A gray light filtered down upon them. The cave was at least ten feet high and, as her eyes adjusted, it appeared to be much larger than Rachel first thought.

"It's a dry cave," Ty uttered. Clucking to his horse, he headed deeper down into the cave. "We've got to try and hide in here until they leave. The farther down we can go, the better off we'll be."

Frantic, Rachel turned around. "Wait!"

Ty halted. He saw her go back out to the mouth of the cave and break off a branch from a cedar tree. Their tracks! *Of course.* He nodded. "Good call."

"You go ahead, I'll sweep our tracks out of here," she said.

Ty kept seeing spots of gray light here and there. He wondered if the top of the cave had holes in it. There had to be holes or he wouldn't be seeing a thing. The cave narrowed at the back. And then it had three different passages he could choose from. Ty waited for Rachel to catch up. "Which one should we try first?" he asked.

His voice echoed hollowly in the cave. She came forward and peered into all three. "Let's take the smallest one, because if they find us, they'll think we took the largest one."

"Good thinking," he praised. Rachel had pulled the fabric off her face. Her skin had a sheen of perspiration. She looked as scared as he felt. "Okay, let's go...."

Chapter 14

At a certain point in the narrowing cave, Ty asked Rachel to tie her horse's reins to the back of his horse's saddle. Though frustrated over the uselessness of his left arm, he couldn't negotiate both animals.

"It's getting narrower as we go," Rachel whispered. She choked down the panic, standing behind the last horse and looking out toward the entrance. Had the Taliban found them? There was no way to know. Her heart beat hard in her chest as she kept both hands on her pistol.

"I know," Ty said, scowling. "We don't have a choice. We're going to have to push forward."

"What if it's a dead end or it gets too narrow?"

"Then we wait it out." Ty knew the rejoinder: if the Taliban found them, they would become easy targets. They'd be dead in seconds.

Rachel wiped her mouth with the back of her hand. "Okay...keep going."

Tugging on the reins, Ty moved forward. Occasionally, a spot of light would appear. He wondered just how many holes were above them. Grateful he could see, he pushed forward as fast as he could. Where did this tunnel end? It was moving upward. Would there be another opening at the end or was it a wall?

Suddenly, Rachel heard men's voices echoing oddly down their corridor. Gasping, she realized they had been found. *Damn!*

"Hurry!" she whispered fiercely. "They've found us!"

Terror arced through him. The floor of the cave was sandy with some pebbles thrown across it. He jerked on the horse's reins and started off at an awkward run. If the Taliban had been able to figure out they were here, despite Rachel trying to cover their tracks, they'd find them in this tunnel, too. The cave floor continued to move upward. The light filtering down became brighter.

Rachel hung back. She heard more yells and cries from the Taliban. They were at the cave tunnel entrances. *Oh God, don't let them find us!* She turned on her heel and raced to catch up with Ty and their horses. Her breath came in sobs. Pressing her hand to her mouth, Rachel knew she couldn't afford to make any more noise.

Ty trotted as fast as the horses would go. They were snorting and fearful. He knew those sounds would echo back through the tunnel, but there was nothing he could do. His boots thunked hard on the surface. More light was ahead. *God, let it be an opening!*

Rachel ran up to her horse. She saw more light

ahead. The cave floor canted steeply upward. It was getting so narrow that the horse's saddles were rubbing against the confining walls. Sweat dripped into her eyes, stinging them. It was hot in the cave. Fear mixed with hope as she trotted behind her horse. She could hear the Talibans' voices. They were getting closer!

Suddenly, shots were fired.

The bullets careened and ricocheted off the walls. Rachel automatically ducked as one whined by her head. The horses bolted, the booming sound scaring them. They lurched forward, panicked.

Ty saw brush ahead. An entrance! The cave suddenly opened up, and both horses lunged past him in order to escape, their eyes rolling in panic. Gripping the reins, Ty hauled back hard on the lead horse. The animal didn't respond, and they crashed through the thick vegetation, branches snapping and leaves exploding around them. The horse was so panicked by the shots that Ty was dragged. He clung on to the reins as he was pulled swiftly through the thickets. He didn't dare let go!

Rachel leaped through the brush, saw Ty jerked off his feet by the charging and frightened lead horse. Making a leap, she managed to grab her own horse's reins. The animal slowed and turned, snorting.

"Ty!" she called.

"I'm okay," he said, clumsily getting to his feet. He cursed softly, yanked off the sling and threw it with disgust to the ground. It was making him off balance, and right now, he'd settle for pain in order to stay on his feet.

More shots shrieked and careened out of the cave.

"Mount up!" he ordered, releasing the knot of the reins from his saddle.

Rachel already had a hand on her scared horse's neck. "Right!" She leaped into the saddle.

Ty did the same. His left arm hurt like hell, but he didn't care. Seeing a small path that led up through the brush, he realized they were on top of a mountain. The path led down and then went upward. He tried to sense where they were.

After he jammed his heels into his frantic horse, Ty guided the frightened animal up through the thickets. They crashed through the underbrush.

Right behind him, Rachel was breathing hard. She held her .45 in her right hand, looking back to see if she saw the Taliban bursting out of the tunnel. *Oh, God, let us get out of this alive!* Her horse lunged, jumped and the brush exploded beneath its legs. They had to get away. Suddenly, they broke out of the thick wall of brush. *There.* She saw a thin trail, probably a goat trail, leading up and over the rise. Slapping the reins to the withers of his sweaty horse, Ty galloped upward, dirt and rock flying behind the scared animal.

Rachel guided her horse right on the rear of Ty's mount. The shooting had stopped. Anxiously looking over her shoulder, she couldn't see the opening anymore. The dense foliage wall hid it. Had the Taliban gotten through it? They must have, she reasoned, and that was why they'd stopped shooting through the tunnel. Fear curled her stomach into a tight, painful fist as she rode hard.

Ty topped the mountain. He jerked his horse to a halt. Rachel came up beside him, her animal dancing and frightened. "Look!" he cried, pointing.

Her jaw dropped. There was only one mountain between them and the village of Samarigam. Not only that, but she saw Emma and Kahlid's Chinook helicopter on the ground. They had to be dropping supplies to the village. And they were too far away for the crew to hear the rifle fire.

"Hold on," she gasped, hauling her horse to a stop. "Let me try this damn radio again!" She thrust her hand into the pocket of her flight suit. Fumbling around, her hand shaking from fear, she finally found it. She yanked it out and gave Ty a desperate look. "Pray this thing is dried out enough to work."

He held his restive horse, his gaze on the radio she held. Rachel's mouth was grim as she twisted the knob that would turn on the radio.

"It works!" she cried. The radio would have enough distance to reach Bravo Base Camp. She quickly placed the call and gave coordinates.

Ty heard a shout behind them. It was the Taliban! "Tell them we're being pursued by Taliban. We've got to make a run for the village right now!"

Nodding, Rachel heard the cries and shouts of angry men nearby. The brush was snapping and popping. They rode their horses through it to reach them. Quickly, she told Ops their position, that the Taliban was chasing them and they needed Apache intervention. Signing off, she jammed the radio back into her thigh pocket. "Let's get the hell out of here!" She clapped her heels to the horse.

They raced over the top of the mountain. The goat trail was thin and narrow. Rachel signaled for Ty to go down the steep, winding path first. She'd stay to the rear. The animals flew down the trail. The danger was in them falling as the rocks were loose and slippery. Ty's horse slid and almost fell. Rachel gulped back a scream as she saw him right the horse and keep heading downward. It was a good thing he came from a cowboy background. He knew how to ride a horse.

Just as they reached the bottom of the trail, Rachel saw the first of the Taliban appear at the top of the mountain. There were too many to count. And they all had their rifles aimed at them. They started firing down at them, the sounds echoing off the nearby mountains. Dirt spat up here and there around them. Turning, Rachel whipped her horse into a gallop. Ty was ahead of her. The mountain connected down a narrow path and then led out, once more, onto the floor of the lush, green valley. Gasping, Rachel felt her horse lose its footing.

In one moment, Rachel was on the horse. The next, the horse slipped and fell. It went head first in a flip. Rachel felt herself sailing through the air. Seconds later, she crashed, rolled into a ball and slammed into the yellow earth. Pain arced up her shoulder, but she kept rolling. She heard the grunt of her horse behind her. Would the horse land on top of her? Uncertain, when she stopped rolling, Rachel sprang to her feet. Eyes wide, she saw her horse only a few feet behind her. It had gotten back on its feet, shaking itself like a dog. She ran back, grabbed the reins and prayed that the horse wasn't injured. Leaping into the saddle, she yelled at the horse and leaned forward.

Instantly, the horse lunged ahead, galloping wildly down the trail. Relieved the horse was unhurt, Rachel found her stirrups. More bullets sang around them. She saw Ty at least half a mile ahead of her. He hadn't realized she had fallen. Rachel leaned down and pushed the horse as fast as he could go. The dust and rocks flew beneath his small, sharp hooves. The bullets kept kicking up geysers of dirt all around her. She was a target!

Rachel knew that Ty was out of rifle range. The last thing she wanted to do was die.

She and her horse burst out of the narrow, dirt path and onto the grassy valley floor. As her horse raced frantically to catch up with his partner, she heaved a sigh of relief. Ty looked back. He had a surprised expression on his face. Rachel signaled for him to keep going, but he slowed down.

It was then that Rachel knew there was more than friendship developing between them. Ty, she was sure, saw how dusty and dirty she looked and knew she had fallen. The look of care on his face touched her as nothing else could. He held his fractious mount back until she could join him.

"I fell," she shouted to him, urging her horse into a gallop. "We're okay! Let's go!"

Ty nodded. Wrenching his horse around, he noted the fifteen Taliban coming down the slope. He cursed and quickly caught up with fleeing Rachel and her mount.

"They're coming after us!" he shouted as he drew abreast of her.

"We'd better hope like hell they got an Apache to cut loose and get it over to us in time, or we're fried."

Now it was a race against death. Rachel kept low in the saddle. She looked back every few strides to see how close the Taliban were. For a while she couldn't see them. Their horses must have tired. She could feel her own mount begin to slow. His coat was covered with sweat and dirt. Up ahead, there was a goat trail that came off from the village above them, but it was a mile long. They had to try and first find it and then climb it. Looking up at the massive, rocky mountain, Rachel's hope began to die. Too much effort and their horses wouldn't last. They had to climb from five thousand to ninety-five hundred feet to Samarigam. If they stayed here, they'd be targets.

Looking up at the sky, the wind tearing past her, Rachel anxiously searched for that black speck that would mean an Apache helicopter was coming their way. But the sky was empty. Without the two Apaches that had been destroyed earlier, BJS was strapped and couldn't send a combat helicopter to every urgent call as much as they might want to. She twisted in the saddle. Her eyes widened. The Taliban had just hit the valley floor. She saw them waving their rifles. Right now, there was two miles between them. And their bullets couldn't reach that far.

"They're on the floor!" she shouted to Ty

He looked back. *Damn!* Twisting back around, he yelled, "We've gotta find that goat trail up to the village!"

Rachel rode up alongside him. Both their horses were wheezing and sucking in huge breaths of air. "I don't know where it is! Do you?"

He shook his head. "We just have to keep riding down the valley until we find it!"

Her hope was shredding as she kept looking back. Was it her imagination or were the Taliban riders getting closer? Their horses might be a lot fresher than their mounts. If that was so, they would slowly but surely close the gap between them. And then they'd start shooting at them. If a bullet hit one of their horses, that would be the nail in their coffins.

"There!" Ty shouted triumphantly. He jabbed his finger toward a trail in the distance.

Rachel noticed the goat trail that led up to the village. It was half a mile away. Her horse was slowing, breath exploding out of his distended nostrils. He was tiring to the point where he would drop from a gallop into a trot. No! Rachel dug her heels into his foaming flanks, but the horse grunted. It lurched forward, wobbling on weakening legs. Up ahead, she saw Ty's horse stagger, its head down, mouth open. They were in serious trouble.

Whipping his horse, Ty forced it back into a gallop. The animal careened drunkenly. And then freezing horror rushed through him. Another group of horsemen galloped toward them from the opposite direction. Taliban or friendly? There was no way to tell. The sky was empty. A horrible, sinking feeling moved through him.

Suddenly, his horse stumbled, and Ty flew out of the saddle.

Rachel gave a cry of terror as she saw Ty's horse collapse beneath him. It hurtled over him and then landed nearby. Yanking her horse to a stop, Rachel leaped off, reins in hand.

"Ty!" He was laying still, arms outstretched, on his belly.

No! Oh, God, no! Let him be alive!

Rachel knelt down and gripped his shoulder. "Ty! Ty, are you all right?"

She lifted her head. Two groups of horsemen came at a high gallop toward them from opposite directions. Gasping, she jerked her attention back to Ty. He was moving.

"Ty! Are you all right? Talk to me."

Groaning, Ty sat up. Blood ran down his left temple. "I'm okay...." He got to his knees and saw his horse lying nearby. The animal had heroically continued until he could go no farther.

Rachel leaped up and yelled, "Come on! We'll ride my horse!" She held out her hand to him.

Within seconds, Ty was back on his feet. He saw the Taliban approaching swiftly. But as he glanced at the southern part of the valley, he saw an equal amount of horsemen would be arriving shortly. His mind spun with what they could do. Rachel jumped into the saddle. She held her hand out, and he swiftly mounted the horse behind her.

"Make a run for the trail!" he yelled.

The echo of gunfire started. Ty knew they were within range of the Talibans' bullets.

Kicking the tired horse, Rachel felt terrible that she was asking the animal to give its all. It lurched into a wobbling trot. The trail was only a quarter of a mile away. The horsemen from the south drew closer and closer. It had to be Taliban. She knew the Taliban were always in touch by phone or cell phone. Chances were, the group chasing them into the cave had called their cohorts, who were already in the valley. Together, they were creating a pincer's movement that would crush them. In a few minutes, they would be dead. The thought scared her as nothing else ever would. The horse was wobbling badly. Suddenly, the animal grunted and collapsed.

Rachel was thrown over the horse's head. She heard the animal hit the ground. Closing her eyes, she rolled after hitting the grass. Stunned, Rachel opened her eyes after she'd stopped moving. The sky was a powdery blue above her. And empty. No Apache was coming to save them. Her heart sank as she scrambled to her feet. She saw Ty lurching up, shaken.

For a moment, they looked at one another. The rifle fire was exploding all around them. A bullet had hit

her horse. That was why it had fallen. And it was dead.
So were they. Gripping the .45, she yelled at Ty, "Get
behind this horse! It's our only cover!"

Leaping behind the body of the horse, they flattened
on their bellies, their pistols drawn. Both had taken the
two extra magazines and laid them nearby. Ty lay so
close he could feel Rachel against him. There wasn't
much cover behind the small, dead horse. Breathing
hard, he positioned his hands on the belly of the animal.

"They're within half a mile. We should wait," Ty
rasped. Otherwise, their bullets could go wild. The
closer the enemy, the better they could aim at them. A
half a mile was too far for their pistols.

"Right," Rachel choked, breathing hard. She jerked
over at Ty. "I want you to know, I forgive you for everything."

The words hit him hard. Ty managed a twisted smile.
Her hair was dirty, her face sweaty, stained with dust.
"Thanks. I think you're one hell of a woman. I'm proud
to be here at your side."

The bullets spit up dust on either side of the horse.
They watched the horsemen from the south start firing,
their rifles winking red and yellow. The Taliban from
the north thundered toward them at high speed.

Rachel choked and sobbed. She held on to Ty's narrowed blue gaze. "I'm sorry," she sobbed. "I'm so sorry,
Ty. I like you.... I was falling in love with you...."

The words slammed into Ty, shocking him. Tears
shimmered in her golden eyes, and her lower lip trembled softly. Yes, he realized, he was falling helplessly
in love with this courageous warrior woman. Reaching
out with his injured left arm, he gripped her shoulder
for a moment. "No matter what happens, just know I
love you, Rachel. I have ever since I met you again...."

Their words to one another were cut off. Several bullets whined overhead. Ty released her shoulder and wrapped his hands around his pistol. Now, they were within target range. He could see the leader, his black eyes filled with hatred, his horse flying toward them, his rifle raised.

Rachel felt her world slowing down to single frames. She had felt this same sensation when she had nearly drowned in the ocean as a child and then during her most recent brush with death. Her whole life was movie slides, and she looked at each one of them. Even though her focus was on the swiftly approaching Taliban, everything seemed to crawl. She saw the saddle leather design on the sweating, foamy horses of the their enemy. She saw each face, the hatred and felt it score her like a bullet would. Mouth tightening, Rachel felt her heart slow down into a powerful, thudding beat. She watched as the horsemen approached. She sighted on the leader. Her hand bucked. The bullet missed him, but it struck his horse. In an instant, the horse crashed to the ground, the leader flying over him. She heard firing next to her. She knew Ty was shooting now, as well. As Ty's bullet took him out and the man went flying out of his saddle, there was a surprised look on his face.

As a bullet whined by her ear, Rachel calmly sighted on another Taliban. She fired two bullets. The second one hit the man who had assumed the lead. The thunder of the horses' hooves now shook the ground. She could feel the reverberation. Every time they fired their pistols, it sounded like major explosions to Rachel. She felt out of her body, every sound amplified painfully against her ringing ears.

A bullet dug into the dead horse they lay behind. Rachel knew that trying to fire accurately from a moving horse was damn near impossible. As the Taliban rode toward them, their bullets flew wildly around them. In comparison, Rachel and Ty's shots were deadly accurate.

By the time the Taliban had arrived, six of the men and two of their horses were dead. Rachel saw the hatred toward them as the Taliban reached within a hundred feet of their position. They were aiming their rifles now, as their horses milled and panicked. She kept on firing. Her hand bucked every time the .45 barked. It felt as if she were in a shooting gallery, her focus only on the enemy she wanted to kill before they killed her.

Ty slammed another magazine into his .38. He heard the slow, systematic crack of Rachel's .45 next to him. He didn't see her, his focus on the enemy now trying to pick them off. The horse's body took so many hits he lost count. Several bullets passed close to his head. Yet, he kept his aim. His training as an Apache gunship pilot allowed him that extraordinary ability. More Taliban fell.

A third Taliban horse went down. The man leaped off, drew his sword and screamed. In a second, he was charging them. Giving a cry, Rachel aimed at the enemy. With one shot, she killed him. He fell two feet in front of their dead horse. Sobbing, she took her last magazine and slammed it into the .45. They were going to die!

Suddenly, Ty saw the Taliban firing over their heads. At what? He twisted around and his eyes rounded. The group of horsemen he'd thought were also Taliban were firing but not at them. At the enemy! Relief sang through him when he realized it must be a friendly group of horsemen, who just happened to be in the valley at the right time.

Turning, he noticed another Taliban soldier whose horse had fallen leap up. This one had an AK-47. He sprayed at them wildly, the bullets flying everywhere. Out of the corner of his eye, he saw Rachel get to her knees, holding her gun out from her body, with both hands, her face a mask of concentration. Her hand bucked once, twice. And then, to his horror, she was shot and flung backwards. With a cry, he leaped to his knees and fired again at the enemy. The AK-47 went flying out of the soldier's hands. A look of genuine surprise that Ty had shot him in the chest crossed his bearded face. The man screamed and fell forward, dead.

Ty was caught in a crossfire as he tried to reach Rachel. She was lying on her back, her eyes half open. The gun had fallen from her nerveless fingers. He couldn't help her. He had to keep firing at the Taliban, who were now making a stand. In the next instant, the horsemen from the south swept up to where he was kneeling and firing. The rest of the Taliban soldiers were killed within moments. Loose, terrified horses ran around wild-eyed and panicked.

Ty recognized the leader, a man on a white Arabian stallion. He was the warlord of the northern Nuristan Province, Rahim Khan. The man was in his forties, with a black beard, dark brown eyes. He gave Ty a triumphant smile.

Turning, Ty leaped to his feet and then fell to his knees at Rachel's side. The air erupted with cries of triumph as the horsemen swirled around the area. His heart pounded with fear as he saw where the bullet had slammed into Rachel's chest, the fabric frayed where it had entered.

"Rachel?" he rasped, leaning over her, his hand on her arm. "Are you okay?" He knew she wore the Kevlar vest. Had it stopped the bullet? Frantically, Ty searched for blood in the area of the wound. He found none. Gasping for breath, his fingers trembling, he touched her pale cheek. "Rachel, look at me."

Slowly, Rachel turned and looked up at him. Her hand moved and she touched her chest. The look in his eyes was one of a man who loved his woman. A man who was frantic with anxiety over her condition. "Damn..." she muttered, touching the bullet hole. "That hurts like hell...."

"You're all right? Any other wounds?" he demanded, looking up. He saw the leader dismount and walk toward them. "Are you okay?" Ty demanded urgently.

"I'll live. Help me up," Rachel said, holding out her hand. Within seconds, Ty's warm, strong hand wrapped around hers. He helped her sit up and then moved his body against her back so she could lean on him.

"The Kevlar stopped the bullet," he said, his lips near her ear as he kept a hand on her slumped shoulder.

Giving a slight chuckle, Rachel said, "Yes, it did."

"So," the leader boomed, "you decided to take on these miserable, flea-bitten dogs alone?"

Rachel looked up, her hand pressed to her chest. "Yes, sir, we did. Thanks for saving us."

"I'm Rahim Khan."

"Yes," Ty told him, his hand on Rachel's shoulder, "we know who you are. Thanks for saving us."

Chuckling, the leader came and knelt down on one knee and critically studied Rachel. "I would say," he murmured with a grin, "that the two of you would probably have won this fight without us."

Rachel shook her head. "No, sir, we wouldn't have." She gestured to the two empty clips near their dead horse. "We were out of ammo."

"It would have been a hand-to-hand combat situation," Ty grimly agreed.

"Still," Rahim said, looking at the bullet hole in Rachel's clothing, "you gave a good account of yourself. What were you doing out here on horseback? I received a call from Bravo Camp that you were out here. We happened to be in the area. In fact, we were coming to meet with Captain Shaheen up at Samarigam. I told your Major Klein that we could render you aid."

Rachel rubbed her chest. The bullet had been stopped by her chicken plate. She would never again curse wearing her Kevlar vest. The stinging sensation was beginning in earnest now and it hurt like hell. "That's why they didn't send an Apache to help us," she told Ty.

Rahim laughed. "No, my friends, that's not true. There were no Apaches to send. They are all assigned to other areas. The major had nothing to help you out." He grinned and thumped his chest. "And so, it came down to us. We might not fly one of those wonderful machines, but I have loyal, faithful men who would follow me to hell and back." He gestured grandly to the men on horseback, who now surrounded them. A booming cheer arose from his comrades.

Ty divided his attention between Rachel and the warlord. He refused to allow her to try and stand up just yet. "We're grateful for your assistance," he told Khan. The leader appeared very pleased.

"Without you," Rachel added, "we wouldn't be here right now."

"Maybe you would be at the gates of heaven," Khan agreed, more serious now.

"How are you feeling?" Ty demanded. Rachel looked pale, her eyes shadowed.

"My chest hurts. It was numb at first, but now it feels like it's on fire."

"No blood, though," he said, again examining her flight suit where the bullet had entered.

"No...just pain. I'll be okay." Rachel glanced up at Ty. Even though her heart was pounding with adrenaline, she felt his care and love. Her mind spun with such shock that it was impossible to deal with it all right then. "We can use my radio and call into base."

Ty nodded and opened the pocket on her left leg. "Yeah, we need to do that."

Rachel felt relief drench her. Khan had an extra mount with him. One of his soldiers brought up the sturdy black horse. It would be their transportation back to the village atop the mountain. She listened to Ty speaking with Major Klein. There was relief in her voice, too. She took a few moments to close her eyes, pushing back the tears. Their families would be notified that they were alive and safe. That would be the best news possible. Sniffing, she opened her eyes. As she looked over at Ty, she swore she saw tears in his eyes, too. But just for a moment. He handed her the radio.

"Feel like standing?"

Holding out her hand, she whispered, "Yes. Let's get to that village."

Ty gently eased her to her feet. Rachel wobbled for a moment. He slid his hand around her shoulders to steady her. She raised her hand and tried to get rid of some of the grass and dust in her hair. So typical of a woman, but his heart swelled with such love for her that he almost cried. They were alive! Once at the horse, which was held by a soldier, he boosted her up onto the saddle. Then he climbed up behind her. In no time, the group left the field of battle and started the steep climb up to Samarigam.

As Ty rode, his arms around Rachel's waist, his whole world was on a tilt. They'd said some things to each other during the heat of battle. The admissions had come pouring out because they thought they were going to die. Did Rachel mean what she'd said? That she *loved* him? The shock of that statement rolled through him. And then he couldn't help admitting that he loved her back. How was all of this possible? How had bitter enemies wound up loving one another? Maybe it was out of shock. When facing death, people did funny things they'd never do in day-to-day life.

Ty was grateful the Khan's men escorted them. Far above, he could see people from the village gathering and watching them approach. They must have seen the battle. Closing his eyes for a moment, he savored Rachel's back resting against him. He could feel the sway and rhythm of the horse beneath them. The sunlight was warm and comforting, the sky a peaceful blue color. So much had happened so quickly. As he studied the sky above them, Ty swore that as soon as things settled down, he had to have private time with Rachel. He had to find out the truth...one way or another.

Chapter 15

As the group of horsemen entered the village of Sa-marigam, Rachel watched people crowd around them and cheer. She turned and grinned at Ty, who sat behind her. He gave her an exhausted smile and nod of his head. Emma and Kahlid were at the edge of the crowd, gesturing for them to ride over. Behind them sat their Chinook helicopter, the crew nearby.

Rachel turned their horse and edged through the crowd. The people smiled, waved and stepped aside so that they could ride toward Emma and Kahlid. When they finally arrived, Rachel dismounted first.

"Rachel!" Emma cried, running up and gripping her shoulders. "Are you all right?"

"I'm fine," she wearily assured her anxious cousin. She couldn't help looking over at Ty and, turning, she noticed how tired he appeared. A dark splotch of blood where he'd been injured before was bleeding again.

"Help me?" she asked Emma and walked over to their horse.

"Ty, let me help you down." Rachel offered her hand up to him.

"Thanks. I'm feeling a little light-headed," Ty admitted. Gripping her hand, he dismounted. If not for her arm going around his waist, he'd have fallen. As he threw his arm around Rachel's shoulders, she steadied him. Kahlid quickly came up.

"Let me help," Kahlid offered, putting his arm around him, as well. Together, they walked him into the bay of the helicopter.

They sat down on the nylon netting that served as a seat. "I'm okay," Ty told Rachel. "Just weak."

Emma said, "We have two doctors and nurses with us. They're in the village today. I'll go get one of them." She trotted out of the helo and disappeared.

Kahlid stood in front of him. "You two almost got killed down there."

"Yeah," Ty muttered, "tell me about it."

"There was nothing we could do except watch. We thought about flying the Chinook down there, but we could have been shot out of the air."

"I know," Ty told the captain. "You couldn't do anything. We needed Apache support, but there was none to be had." He saw the worry in the Afghan officer's eyes. "We got lucky with Lord Khan being in the area."

Nodding, Kahlid murmured, "Yes. I called BJS at Camp Bravo and informed the major that he was on his way here. He has some health problems and was going to meet with the docs here today."

"Good timing," Ty said. He closed his eyes. "I've

ripped open that wound on my left arm again. I'm bleeding like a stuck pig...." And that was the last thing Ty remembered.

When Ty regained consciousness, the first thing he saw was Rachel at his side. He felt her warm hand on his gowned shoulder. Slowly the room came into focus before his blurred vision. The room was surrounded by olive-green curtains. There was an IV in his right arm.

"You're okay, Ty," Rachel soothed, leaning over him and seeing if he recognized her. "You passed out from loss of blood. Kahlid and Emma flew you straight to Bagram Air Base outside of Kabul. You got a transfusion, and a surgeon fixed up your left arm. How are you feeling?" Rachel gently squeezed his shoulder. As he slowly moved his head and looked up at her, she gave him a wobbly smile of welcome.

"B-bagram?" His throat was dry, parched.

"Yes, you're safe. We're home, Ty. You're going to be okay. Are you thirsty?"

She must be a mind reader, Ty thought. Giving a slight nod, he tried to lick his dry lips without success.

Rachel took a glass that had water and a glass straw in it from the bed stand. She guided the straw between his cracked lips. "Drink..." she quietly urged.

The water tasted wonderful. He drank two glasses before he was sated. The water cleared his sluggish mind. Other sounds filtered into his consciousness. Men and women talked in quiet voices outside his curtained cubicle. The smell of anesthesia was everywhere, along with bleach and alcohol odors. Looking down at himself, he saw that he was dressed in a blue gown. His dirty flight uniform was gone. As Rachel came and sat down at his bedside, he asked, "How long have I been here? What happened?"

Rachel looked at her watch. "After you passed out, it took us an hour to fly to Bagram. Kahlid had called ahead. When we got here, there was a team waiting. You took over two pints of blood. The doctor who worked on your arm said you probably tore an artery during our firefight and said you were bleeding to death." Mouth quirking, Rachel managed a pained smile. "You went into cardiac arrest after arriving here. They had to revive you with the paddles twice before you started breathing again."

"I almost died?"

"Yes, from blood loss." Rachel leaned forward and kissed his sweaty brow. "I almost lost you, Ty, before I'd found you." Tears welled in her eyes and she seemed embarrassed. Sniffing, she wiped them away.

Nothing shattered Ty so much as a woman crying. He could barely contain his own emotional reaction to her tears. When her lips met his brow, Ty felt such life and warmth in her grazing touch. For a moment, he closed his eyes and wrestled with his own feelings. He'd nearly died. *Oh, God...* Ty opened his eyes and gazed up at her. She was still in her dirty flight uniform, her hair mussed with bits of grass and dust. Her face was smudged. She was the most beautiful sight to him.

"I didn't know...." he managed hoarsely.

"It was touch and go for a while," Rachel shakily assured him. She moved her hand gently across his broad shoulder. "But you're going to be fine now. The E.R. doc said the reason your heart cavitated was because there wasn't enough blood in the chambers. As soon as they got the transfusion into you, your heart was fine."

"And you were there and saw it?"

"Yes. They ordered me out, but I refused to go. I... wanted to be with you, Ty. We'd gone through so much together. We fought for our lives down in that valley, and we were vastly outnumbered. The least I could do was be at your side." Rachel blinked back more tears. "I—I love you, Ty. I know we said it to one another in the heat of battle, but I meant it."

Holding her tearful golden gaze, Ty saw how her lower lip trembled. How badly he wanted to hold her. Love her. Right now, he felt so weak that it was tough just to raise his good arm. His left arm was swathed in a bandage and in a sling across his chest. He moved his hand. It was painful, but he didn't care. His fingers covered her other hand resting on the side of his bed.

"Listen," he told her, his voice rough with emotion, "I meant it, too, Rachel. I don't know when or how it happened. All I know is that it did." Searching her teary gaze, Ty added, "We've just gone through hell and we've survived it. We need time to get to know one another. Time to heal up from what we just experienced together."

Rachel gently enclosed his fingers, which were cold to the touch. Ty's face was no longer pasty, but he didn't look terribly healthy, either. The doctor who had saved his life had warned her he'd be dazed for at least another twenty-four hours. "I want time with you, Ty. Our past is gone. I'm glad to release it." She smiled softly, searching his blue eyes. "There's just so much about you that is heroic and good."

His heart swelled with a fierce love for her. "I'm no hero," Ty muttered. "I was a villain of the worst kind in the past. I have a lot to make up for, Rachel. I'm grateful you'll let me try."

"You are a hero, Ty," Rachel whispered. "In *my*

eyes. My heart." Standing up, her hand still holding his, she leaned over and gently placed her lips against his. Ty's mouth was strong against hers. Drowning in the moment she'd long dreamed of, Rachel lifted her other hand and caressed his stubbled cheek. He might be feeling weak due to all his trials, but his mouth was cherishing against hers. She absorbed the warmth of his moist breath, the joy shared between them in finding one another. Slowly, regretfully, Rachel eased her lips away. She smiled into Ty's darkened blue eyes. "I need to go get cleaned up. There are shower facilities here. When I come back, Emma and Kahlid will be here."

Nodding, Ty gripped her fingers. The pain of the needle in his arm was erased by his fierce love after her wonderful kiss. "Okay, get cleaned up. I'll be waiting."

Rachel straightened and carefully unwound her fingers from his. "I'll be back in an hour," she promised.

Shortly afterward, her heated kiss lingering on his mouth, Ty dropped off into a deep, healing sleep. He had closed his eyes, simply feeling Rachel's soft lips grazing his. He had silently promised her as he spiraled downward that somehow, he'd make it all up to this heroic, courageous woman. She deserved his love, respect and admiration. And then Ty had known no more.

When Ty awakened, Emma and Kahlid were sitting on either side of his bed. He slowly sat up, feeling stronger. Emma stood and placed extra pillows behind his back.

"Welcome back to the land of the living," Kahlid told him with a grin.

"Thanks," Ty said. He looked around his enclosed cubical. "Where's Rachel?"

"She'll be here in a minute," Emma assured him, sitting back down.

Emma's red hair was shoulder length and framed her face. Ty saw that she was in her NGO, non-government organization, blue flight suit. "What time is it?" he asked.

"It's 1700," Kahlid told him. "We got here about fifteen minutes ago." He smiled over at his wife. "I had some tactics and strategies to discuss with your doctor first."

Emma grinned and touched Ty's hand. "Kahlid knows the generals," she told him. "And sometimes, that's a plus."

Confused, Ty looked at them. He was about to speak when Rachel slipped through the curtains. The change in her was shocking. Instead of her dark green flight suit, she was dressed in a pair of white slacks, a dark blue top with a white jacket over it. Her hair had been washed and dried. It hung straight and shining around her shoulders.

"How are you feeling?" Rachel asked, coming over and pressing a kiss to his brow.

"Better, now that you're here," Ty told her, managing a slight smile. Rachel's face shone and her cheeks were flushed, her gold eyes gleaming with love toward him. Ty had never felt such love before in his life. And like a beggar, he greedily lapped it up. "How are you?"

"Clean." Rachel laughed.

Emma and Kahlid joined her.

"You look beautiful in civilian clothes," Ty said. Indeed, he'd never seen Rachel in them before. Her cheeks turned a bright red, which only enhanced her natural beauty.

"Thanks," she said shyly. Standing at his bedside, Rachel placed her hand on his right shoulder. "You must have just woke up?" she guessed.

Rubbing his face, Hamilton muttered, "Yes. How long was I out?"

"An hour," she told him. Rachel looked at her cousin. "Did you tell him what Kahlid managed to wrangle from the general?"

Shaking her head, Emma said, "No, we thought you'd like to tell Ty."

Frowning, Ty looked at them. They were all grinning like cats that had some secret shared among them. "Okay," he said, looking up at Rachel, "what's going down?"

"How would you like to come with me to their home in Kabul?" Rachel asked. "It's a huge villa up on a hill, and it's guarded 24/7. Emma and Kahlid are giving us the wing that has two suites with adjoining doors. We're going to be their guests for the next three days. Kahlid managed to get the days off from the general. They're good friends. Plus, your doctor said you couldn't go back to flight duty for at least two weeks. And he's signed off on three days off base for you because of your injury."

"And," Emma said in a conspiratorial whisper, "the general authorized the two of you to stay at our home. Isn't that great?"

Rachel laid her hand on Ty's shoulder. "What do you think about this?" She didn't want him to feel pressured. Judging from the relief in his eyes, she knew Ty was fine with the decision.

"It's important you're okay with this," he said to Rachel.

"I'm fine," she murmured. Her heart opened, and she felt such an incredible rush of warmth toward Ty.

"We need the time," he agreed. Looking over at the couple, Ty said, "Thanks a lot."

Emma smiled and slid her arm around her tall, lean husband. He drew her near. "In a war zone, you don't get a lot of uninterrupted quality time just to talk."

"And that's exactly what we need," Ty said, giving Rachel a hopeful look. He didn't know where the three days would lead them, but that wasn't important.

Rachel squeezed his shoulder. "I've already called my parents and contacted my sisters. They know I'm okay."

"Good," Emma said, leaning her head against Kahlid's broad shoulder. "Because at the first opportunity, I'd called them myself."

"I know and I'm glad you did. My mom was beside herself. You saved her a couple of hours of waiting for my phone call."

"I'm sure the Army notified my father," Ty commented sourly.

Rachel patted his shoulder gently. "At least he knows you're alive." The stubbornness in his eyes gave away just how resistant he was to talking with his estranged father. She hoped that someday Ty could get past his anger for what his father had done to him. His jaw clenched. Forgiveness was a long road.

Emma said, "There's a wonderful housekeeper who will be there if you need anything. Kahlid's driver, Nabi, will take you home."

Kahlid pressed a kiss to his wife's red hair. "And

we'll be there shortly. My housekeeper doesn't speak English, but we'll be around."

"And you're welcome to join us at dinner," Emma told them. "Or if you want to take your dinner in your suites, that's fine, too. Whatever is comfortable for you."

Rachel said, "Cousin, you rock. Thank you."

Ty grinned. "I'd like to get out of this gown, get into some civilian clothes and leave all this behind." He held up his arm that had the IV taped to it.

Laughing, Rachel said, "I'll get the nurse. You've already been signed out."

"You and I are about the same height," Kahlid said, releasing his wife. "I put some of my clothes in the locker down the hall. They'll probably fit."

"Thanks. I'll make them fit." Ty gave the gown a distasteful look. "I'm not happy running around in this thing."

Chuckling, Emma took Kahlid's hand and tugged him toward the curtains. "Come on, Kahlid. We still have work to do."

"Nabi will come here to your cubicle in about twenty minutes," Kahlid said.

"I'll wait for him," Rachel said. She felt giddy inwardly, as if floating on air. She and Ty would have some quiet downtime to talk. That's what was needed now more than anything. Good, deep talks. Who knew where it would lead?

Ty couldn't believe the luxury of his suite. The driver had delivered them to the hilltop estate. It was completely surrounded by a ten-foot fence with concertina wire on top. Plus, four guards constantly patrolled the area. It was, according to chatty Nabi, one of the few homes that the Taliban had not destroyed. Ty felt safe knowing the security measures that Kahlid had taken. His arm was still in a sling. And he was grateful that Kahlid's jeans, a dark blue polo shirt and socks all fit. He was still wearing his flight boots. A fashion plate, he was not.

The suite consisted of three rooms. The first was a living room, the second a massive bathroom. On the other side of it was a room with a king-size bed with a colorful quilt thrown across. Everywhere he looked, he saw Americana. He knew Kahlid had gotten his degree at Princeton University and was steeped in American culture. As he stood looking at the overstuffed couches and chairs, Ty felt at home.

There was a light tap on his door. Turning, he called, "Come in...."

Rachel poked her head around the door. "Hey, this is like a five-star hotel! I wanted to see your digs. Do you mind?"

Smiling, Ty said, "No, not at all." Just seeing the tension easing from Rachel's face made his heart expand with joy. "What's your place like?"

"Kahlid loves quilts," Rachel said as she entered his suite. "And my whole place is decorated with quilts, framed or otherwise. Yours reminds me more of a 1930s decor you'd find in the Midwest." She went over and touched the cherry rocker that had a small quilt hanging over the back.

"I'm not that up on decorations," Ty said, frowning. He saw that there was hot tea and two cups sitting on the coffee table. "Want some tea?" he asked.

Rachel brightened. "I'd love some!" It felt wonderful to just share time and space with Ty. She saw him struggling to do the right thing. After their past, he was trying desperately to make her feel welcome. She walked over and said, "Why don't you take a seat in that overstuffed chair. I'll pour."

Grateful, Ty sat down. "It feels good to sit," he admitted.

Rachel noted his face was pale. His eyes were shadowed. Pouring the fragrant tea into the delicate china cups, she said, "The nurse said you're going to need a solid, uninterrupted night's sleep to feel like your old self again."

Ty took the cup and saucer from her. There was nothing but grace about Rachel. Her hair was now washed, dried and shone like an ebony frame around her beautiful face. "I feel like I'm in some kind of dream," he murmured, tasting the tea.

Sitting down on the couch opposite him, Rachel sipped her tea. "It's hard going from this to a war zone not more than half a mile from your house." She appreciated his clean, brown hair, a rebellious lock fell over his brow.

"I don't know how Kahlid and Emma do it. They're out there flying to border villages every day. And they're wide open to attack. No Apache escorts for them because they're an NGO."

"My cousin is like all of the Trayherns," Rachel said, balancing the cup on her crossed legs. "We're adaptable, flexible and from the earliest time we can remember taught that life throws curveballs at us. My parents raised all of us girls to be able to shift and make the necessary changes."

Ty raised his brows. "The more I hear about your parents, the more I wish I had a set of them instead."

Losing some of her smile, Rachel felt deeply for Ty. She could see the hurt, the old anger and confusion that his father had created within him. "Your father wasn't a model parent," she quietly agreed. "But he did the best he could, Ty."

"Not damn good enough," he growled.

"You've changed despite him," Rachel coaxed in a soft tone, holding his murky stare. "And you need to give yourself credit for that, Ty. You are not your father."

"Not any longer." He absorbed the kindness in her gaze. "Rachel, I want to make up for what I did to you. You took the brunt of my misguided anger."

Her mouth lifted a little. "You're doing it right now, Ty. Don't you see that?"

"It's not enough."

"I don't want you doing anything out of guilt." There was a glint in her eyes.

"Not to worry on that point. When I first saw you at Fort Rucker, before I knew you were in pilot training, I thought I'd met an angel, died and gone to heaven." He saw the surprise in her expression. "You were as beautiful then as you are now."

Blinking, Rachel said, "I don't remember meeting you before I was assigned to your class."

"I saw you at the base hospital. There was a drive for blood, and you were standing in line."

"I had forgotten about that. Yes, I was there. Where were you?"

"I'd just given blood and was going out the other set of doors. You didn't see me." His voice lowered. "But I saw you."

"It must have been a shock for me to show up in your class."

"Yes, it was. A part of me just wanted to fall all over you like a lovesick teenager. Another part kept hearing my father's words that women were weak."

"Well," she sighed, "we know which part won out."

"Too bad the teen didn't." He gave her a hopeful look. Rachel didn't seem as upset about the past as he felt.

"Yes, I'd much rather have dealt with your attention that way." She grinned a little. "It's nice to know the rest of the story, Ty. Thank you."

His conscience eased over the words and the sincere expression in her eyes. "I didn't want to hate you, Rachel. I wanted to get to know you. I felt torn with you in the class. Later, I realized the truth about why I was so cruel."

"I was your whipping post," she agreed.

"Not anymore." Ty gave her a heated look charged with meaning. "I need to hear it again. Did you mean what you said out there in the valley? That you loved me? Or was that said in fear and knowing you were going to die soon?"

"I meant it. I wanted you to know how I really felt about you, Ty, before we died."

"When did you know?" he wondered.

"What? That I loved you?" Rachel looked up at the ceiling and then back at him. There was an incredible peace in his face now, as if some huge load had dissolved from his shoulders. He'd carried his father long enough. "When I realized you weren't going to come after me like you did at Fort Rucker. I got to see the other side of you, Ty. What I call your good side." She smiled impishly. "I felt like I was rediscovering you all over again. And I liked what I saw. I allowed myself to open up to you, Ty. You didn't know it, but I was watching you closely. I wanted to see if the 'new' Ty Hamilton was there all the time or his evil twin was going to sneak back in."

Laughing a little, Ty felt warm all over. The joy, the elfin quality dancing in Rachel's golden eyes made him feel ten times the man he was minutes ago. She made him feel good, he realized. "My evil twin is no more," he promised her in a deep voice.

"I know that now. For sure." Rachel's smile dissolved. "When we were out there in the valley and the Taliban was galloping down upon us, I knew we'd die." She moved the cup gently around in her hands, staring at the brown tea inside it. For a long moment, she didn't speak. Finally, Rachel lifted her head and tried to put how she felt into words. "I wanted you to know I'd forgiven you. And that somewhere along the line, I had fallen so deeply in love with you...."

Chapter 16

Rachel felt like taking a dip in the hot tub. She'd just awakened from her nap after having lunch with Ty. Looking at her watch, she saw it was nearly 3:00 p.m. The sun was slanting through the floor-to-ceiling windows, brightening her suite. Emma had urged them to take advantage of the hot tub while at the villa. Rachel was still sore from the earlier helicopter crash. And she'd taken Emma's advice and used the heat to help her tightened muscles. This was their last day here at the villa. Tomorrow morning, Nabi would drive them back to Bagram Air Base and they'd fly the new Chinook assigned to them back to Bravo. Life would once more become tense and dangerous.

With a softened sigh, Rachel shimmied out of her clothes, walked into the bathroom, grabbed a bright yellow towel and wrapped it around herself. The hot tub was only about ten feet down the hall. Opening the door, she looked both ways. For a split second, she almost walked up the hall to Ty's room to invite him to join her. Rachel felt scared and hesitated. They'd talked every chance they got. Their most important conversations lasted deep into each night. Starving to explore Ty, Rachel felt her love growing for this man. She knew no human being on earth was perfect, that they had all made mistakes, large and small. Her hand tightened on the top of her towel, which hid her body. Should she go ask Ty to join her?

Nervous, Rachel decided not to do it. She was afraid of herself. Afraid that Ty might reject her, no matter how close she felt to him. He had so much to overcome. And she felt they'd come a long way in a very short amount of time. As she padded down the carpeted hall toward the spa room, she waffled. How she wanted Ty. All of him and in every way. In her nightly dreams, she made passionate love with him. Even now, the memories brought heat into her face. During their talks, she'd seen the hunger and need for her in his eyes, too. But Ty hadn't made a move, either. Maybe they were both too scared, the past hovering threateningly over them.

Yes, that was it, Rachel decided. They had such a past history of hurt that they were frightened to death of making a mistake that could destroy their fragile new relationship. They both wanted it so bad that they were afraid to make the first move. Mouth tightening, Rachel placed her hand on the brass doorknob and opened the door that led to the huge, round hot tub.

"Oh!"

Ty was sitting in the hot tub. His eyes widened considerably as Rachel entered and then froze on the spot.

"I didn't know," he began lamely, trying to make her feel at ease. He was sitting on the granite bench, the water up to his torso, his dark-haired chest exposed. Seeing the redness sweep across her cheeks, Ty realized she was embarrassed to find him so obviously naked. His muscles were aching, and the hot water helped them relax.

"I'm sorry," Rachel stumbled, her hand still on the doorknob.

"Wait. Don't go," he called. "Come on in." Suddenly, Ty's fear of rejection dissolved. He held his hand out to her. "I'd like you to come in with me, if you want...?"

Moistening her lips, Rachel hesitated. Ty's hair was wet and gleaming. His naked upper body glistened. He was so incredibly ripped. At the base camp, she'd seen him work out at least an hour a day in the gym. "Well... I...I didn't know you'd be in here." The words came out whispered and halting to her. The hope burned in his face, those large, intelligent blue eyes of his narrowing like a laser—on her. Instantly, her body responded. She felt her breasts firming, her nipples tightening. It was a hungry look, of a man wanting his woman. Even her lower body responded to Ty's heated, dangerous stare.

Her fear vanished. It was a relief, because right now, all Rachel really wanted was to be in Ty's arms. Turning, she shut the door—and then locked it. No way did she want the housekeeper accidentally coming in to surprise them. Kahlid and Emma were on a flight. They had the villa to themselves. Turning, she said, "I don't need this, do I?" She allowed the yellow towel to drop to her feet.

Ty suppressed a gasp and felt pure awe as Rachel stood naked near the door. She was statuesque, her shoulder thrown back, her chin tilted at a proud angle. "No," he rasped, standing up. "You don't. Come here...." He walked across the large, round hot tub to where the stairs were located.

She let her gaze rake his taut, muscular body. The water pooled just below his hips, and she could see that he wanted her. A slight, careless smile fled across her mouth as she walked over to him. Without a word, Rachel took his proffered hand and walked down the four steps and into the warm, swirling water. Ty released her hand, his arms sweeping about her, drawing her hard against him.

The air rushed out of her lungs as he claimed her. Rachel smiled and moved her hands upward to frame his damp face. His blue eyes burned with a hunger that intensified her own need of him. "I want you, Ty. All of you, in every way," Rachel whispered, leaning upward, her mouth claiming his. She drank in his powerful need of her.

Ty led her to the center of the bubbling water. Their bodies were locked tightly against one another. He could feel the swell of her breasts, the hard nubs of her nipples pressing into his chest. Her hips were rounded and soft compared to his angular hips. When her arms entwined around his thick neck, her fingers moving though the short strands of his black hair, Ty groaned. Yesterday he'd gotten rid of the sling. His left arm was sore, but useable. The water created a silken movement between them.

As Ty broke their heated kiss, he guided his hand upward and slid his fingers through her hair. Rachel moaned and tipped her head back, eyes closed. Her hands were busy roving slickly across his back, touching him, exploring him. Her breath came in gasps just as his did. In moments, he led her down into the warm water. It was hot because of the summer heat, but it felt embracing.

Rachel smiled up at him as he took her down into the bubbling, blue water. His return smile devastated her hungry senses. Focusing on his very male mouth, she reached out and traced his flat lower lip with her index finger. As Ty settled them on the underwater bench, she floated across his lap. Her body situated against his, she could feel his need of her. Raw desire exploded through her. Lifting her arms, she placed them around Ty's neck, and she kissed him hard.

Her mouth was wreaking fire from his lips down to his burning lower body. With each movement, Ty felt himself coming unraveled. Her mouth was wet and hot as she kissed his brow, his closed eyes, cheek, and finally, his mouth once more. Tunneling his fingers into her hair, he angled her such that he could plunder her mouth as never before as her hands drifted in exploration across his chest. And then she broke the kiss and moved away from him.

Ty knew there were several dark blue pads laying next to the hot tub. They were made of thick foam rubber and comfortable. As Rachel went toward the stairs, he held her hand. She smiled teasingly at him, which sent a bolt of powerful heat through him. There was no disguising she wanted him as much as he wanted her.

"Come here," Ty rasped, drawing her close. "Let's get out and lay on this." He pointed to it.

Rachel's smile grew. "How handy to have them."

Grinning, Ty led her out of the hot tub. "It's perfect for us…. Come on…." He led her up the stairs and onto the soft pads.

Without hesitation, Rachel laid down next to Ty. Her

hair was damp, the ends sticking against her glistening shoulders. His face was like that of a raptor: intense and focused. The air escaped her lips as Ty turned her onto her back and slid his hand beneath her neck. His head dipped and Rachel closed her eyes in anticipation. His mouth sought her hardened nipples, one after another. As he suckled her, laved his tongue across them, her entire body convulsed with pleasure. The power of the movement sent a scalding heat into her lower body. Moaning, Rachel couldn't stand the teasing any longer. Reaching up, she pulled Ty over her. Looking up into his narrowed eyes, she whispered, "Love me. Take me with you...." She thrust her hips upward to meet and meld with him.

Gritting his teeth, Ty felt her capture him. In moments, she had pulled him deep within her moist, heated confines. Her hands slid over his hips, trapping him and then moving slowly with a rhythm that shattered his mind. No longer was Ty thinking. They were reacting wildly, like the primal animals they'd suddenly shifted into and become. Leaning down, he caught and captured Rachel's parted lips, shifting her on top of him. His hands moved to either side of her head, and he groaned as they established a violent, stormy rhythm. The world dissolved into a boiling cauldron they shared between them. The movements were swift and hard. He heard Rachel's breath come in sobs, felt her fingers digging frantically into his bunched shoulders. Closing his eyes, Ty surrendered himself to her powerful, womanly core. For the first time, he allowed her love to completely envelop him.

His world slowed, burned, and Ty absorbed her fierce love for him. He felt his heart opening. It was such a strange and startling sensation, but it didn't pull him out of that cloud of euphoria. Like the starving man he was, he realized in some small, functioning part of his brain that Rachel loved him with her life. Indeed, she'd knelt at his side, firing at the charging Taliban who were intent on killing them. Rachel had shown such courage under fire. And now, she was sharing herself, her hungry body with him. Fully. No reservations. As his hands settled across her hips, he sank even more deeply into her. Ty heard her gasp with pleasure, and he plunged into a blanket of fire that roared through him. In moments, he felt himself explode within her. Simultaneously, Rachel suddenly stiffened and uttered a deep moan. His world tumbled end over end in a fire that consumed both of them. Ty felt his heart widening and love pouring through him as they collided like fiery stars into one another. Suddenly, they both froze as if paralyzed.

Rachel felt his entire body contract, his hands grip her hips as he growled and released. They were like two animals locked with one another, hungry, starving and now being sated by one another. Eyes closed, Rachel had never felt such raw pleasure as now. Ty caressed her as she lay down across him, her head nestled against the curve of his neck. All Rachel could do was sob and feel the liquid fire of her body collapsing in on itself. His fingers moved in grazing touches across her back, following the curve of her spine and caressing her silky hair.

Absorbing Rachel's relaxed body against his, Ty lay there, feeling satiated as never before. He didn't want to open his eyes yet. He simply wanted to feel the heavy warmth of Rachel upon him, the burning power of them connected with one another, her moist, ragged breath upon his shoulder. A smile pulled at his mouth as he continued to trace and memorize her shoulders, arms and back. Her hips were flared, and as his hands cupped them, he felt another powerful urge. The urge to procreate, to give her a child. Their child. In those stunning moments, Ty knew that any baby that they may have created now or in the future would be raised with love, not fear and beatings. His fingers grazed her hips, and he absorbed those powerful possibilities.

Rachel lifted her head from the crook of his shoulder. She smiled down at Ty. He had such love mirrored in his eyes for her that she felt as if the entire world had shifted. Rachel touched his cheek. "It was incredible," she whispered. "I've never felt so satisfied as right now...."

Those were the words he needed to hear. Ty realized he was still emotionally fragile with Rachel. His heart loved her with an undying fierceness, and he was playing catch-up with the stunning turn of events. Lifting his hand, he guided her so that she sat up on him. Her hair was tangled and mussed, her lips soft and pouty from their shared kisses. As her hands rested on his chest, her fingernails trailed and tangled softly in his dark hair. Ty liked the gold glimmer in her half-closed eyes, a lioness satiated. Lifting his hands, he cupped her breasts and moved his thumbs across her hardening nipples. She gave him a predatory smile.

"I'm not done with you, Ty."

Leaning up, Ty rocked her so that his knees were a support for her back. "I'm not, either," he growled, leaning over and suckling one of her nipples.

Rachel sighed and moaned, curving her arms around his broad shoulders. Everything was so right. So natural between them. The heat built in her breasts and then traveled like a line of igniting fire down through the center of her body. She felt the power of him moving suggestively within her. A sigh of pleasure whispered from her lips as he reminded her of their connection.

Rachel leaned back against his drawn up legs and savored his masculine hardness, his unmerciful teasing. His mouth traveled from one nipple to the other, inciting them, fanning the flames once more. Surprised at how quickly her body wanted Ty all over again, she opened her eyes and then gently pushed him down on the mat.

"My turn," she whispered, and she began to rock her hips forward and back with intensity.

Hands against her hips, Ty felt her power, a woman taking her man. It was something beautiful to experience, not control over one another but a sharing of that raw gift of love between them. Indeed, he saw her lips part and felt her entire body contract around him. Rachel threw her head back, exposing the beautiful curve of her neck. Her fingers dug deeply into his flesh as they once more experienced a simultaneous orgasm. The rippling heat moved against him, and he gasped with pleasure as, once more, he released into her scalding confines. For a moment, their eyes closed. Imprisoned within the heat of their passion, Ty felt his world spinning out of control.

He was in a dive that he never wanted to recover from. Never in his life had he experienced what he was sharing with Rachel right now. The world had turned over, inside out, and he was like a butterfly being born out of the imprisonment of a cocoon. It wasn't a painful sensation; it was beautiful, and life began to flow through him as never before. Now, Ty understood when someone said that love had changed them completely. Rachel's love had changed him forever and in a good way. He was finally free of his past, because she loved him enough to walk with him into an unknown future together.

Groaning, Rachel fell against Ty, spent and weak. Her head lay on his shoulder, and she relished the feel of his arms wrapped around her, simply holding her safe against his male body. She felt each breath he took, body and soul. Trailing her hand gently across Ty's left shoulder, she was always aware of his bandaged wound. She lifted her head and placed several moist kisses on that broad shoulder that had carried so many loads alone for far too long. She licked his flesh, tasted the salt of him. He groaned with pleasure as she continued her exploration across his skin. Smiling to herself, she inhaled his male scent. It was all good. She loved Ty with a fierceness that took even her by surprise. And yet, Rachel felt content as never before.

Easing off him, Rachel moved down to his side and snuggled into his awaiting arms. The humid warmth of the hot-tub room was a wonderful blanket. The late afternoon sunlight poured into the western, stained-glass windows, making it seem like the rainbow lived where they lay. She opened her eyes and caressed Ty's damp hair. Rachel drowned in his glinting blue gaze. His face had never looked so relaxed or peaceful. "I love you, Ty. With my heart, my soul. I never want to be apart from you...."

Ty heard the trembling and husky words slipping from her well-kissed mouth. He grazed her lips and whispered, "I love you with my heart, my soul, Rachel...."

For a long time, they lay in one another's arms. The bubbling sounds of the hot tub, the rainbow colors dancing around the room, all served to make their love something magical for Rachel. She was content to lay against Ty's strong, powerful body. Absorbing his tender touches, Rachel wanted to memorize every inch of him.

Finally, reality intruded upon them. Ty watched the sun leave the windows and the rainbows dissolved. The entire afternoon had been one of kisses, exploration, joy and sharing. "I don't ever want this to end," Ty admitted, his voice raspy.

Closing her eyes, Rachel murmured, "Me neither. This is so magical, Ty. Stepping into this room was like stepping into another world. A world where there is no fighting and killing. Only hope." She opened her eyes and held his tender gaze. "Here, we could love one another and not worry about the violent world around us." She touched his cheek. "And I know tomorrow morning, we're going back into that other world."

His brows fell as he saw worry shadow her golden eyes. With his index finger, Ty traced each of her brows. "Love has seen us this far," he whispered, "and it will see us the rest of the way."

Rachel nodded, her brows tingling with pleasure. "I know," she said. "But, I don't want this to end. We've just found one another, Ty."

He heard the worry in her husky voice. Drawing her deep into his arms, he simply held her. "When someone would tell me love conquers all, I always laughed and made fun of them. That was because," Ty said next to her ear, "I had never been in love before. Now, I am, and I understand what the guy was trying to share with me." He kissed her hair. "Love will see us through this year, Rachel. We'll weather whatever happens because we do love one another. Make sense?"

Rachel left his arms and sat up. Ty joined her, his

arm sliding around her shoulders and drawing her close. There was something about being naked with him that made Rachel feel safe and wanted. And he was so beautiful to look at, the dangerous gleam in his eyes, the predator who wanted to stalk her all over again. Her body responded heatedly to his intent stare. "It does make sense, Ty. We've gone through so much since we met again. We not only had to deal with our collective past with one another, but we're in a war, too."

Nodding, Ty whispered, "We have the time, sweet one." He reached out and touched her knee, then added, "There's no hurry about us. We'll be at the same base. We can see one another every time we can make it happen."

"At least I'll be with your squadron for the next five months."

Ty leaned forward and cupped her face. He wanted to erase the worry and anxiety he saw in Rachel's narrowing eyes. "Listen to me. Even though you will go back to BJS and flying the Apache, we'll find spaces and places to be with one another."

"I don't want to lose what we have," she admitted. "I fell in love before, and Garrett was killed."

Ty drew Rachel back into his arms. She rested her head against his right shoulder. "The past is the past. It's not going to repeat," Ty promised her, lips near her ear. After kissing her cheek, he made Rachel look up at him. "If we can surmount our past, don't you think there's a greater plan at work here? We didn't meet again to carry on our war with one another. We met because it was time for us to heal our wounds. And because we have, Rachel, we're going to get the reward of loving one another fully. For a long, long time."

His words made so much sense to her. Slipping her

arms around his shoulders, she whispered, "Thank you, Ty. I hadn't thought of it like that."

"We're being given a second chance with one another, Rachel." Looking deep into her sleepy gaze, he said, "And I'm grateful. We have nowhere to go but up with one another. We were as far down as two people can get five years ago."

Rallying to his optimism, she smiled. "You've come so far and grown so much, Ty. I'm in this for the long term, too. I like what we have. I love talking with you. You're an incredible man, and you inspire me in so many ways."

"I feel the same about you," Ty admitted with a grin. Looking up, he saw the sky was beginning to lose its bright, powdery blue color. "Let's take a shower together. Then we can get dressed and tell the housekeeper we're having dinner with Emma and Kahlid tonight. It's our last night here, and I'd like to thank them for their kindness."

"Good idea," Rachel said. "But one more kiss…" She leaned upward and met his smiling mouth. Ty tasted so good to her, his lips commanding against her own. And once more, she felt the fire ignite in her lower body. Breaking the kiss, Rachel laughed breathlessly. "I can't even kiss you, Ty Hamilton, without wanting to love you all over again!"

Ty got to his feet and pulled Rachel into his arms. "You don't have to look far to see what your kiss did to me."

Grinning wickedly, Rachel could see his arousal once more. "I have a feeling that we're not going to have much sleep tonight."

"Me, too," Ty gloated, picking up her towel and handing it to her.

Rachel wrapped the towel around her glowing body and watched as he put his own around his narrow hips. "I want to tell my folks about us. Are you okay with that?"

"Sure." Ty walked over and squeezed her. "The time over here isn't going to work against us, Rachel. I feel the year we share here will be good for us."

Nodding, she walked with him toward the door. "I'm thinking of getting married after we get back home." She searched his peaceful-looking features. Did he feel the same?

"I'd like that," Ty said, kissing her hair. Leaning forward, he unlocked the door. "And I love you...."

Emma was all smiles at the dinner table after Rachel had told them of their plans to marry after they finished with their tour. "That's wonderful!"

"Don't call your parents yet," Rachel warned with a laugh as she drank her after-dinner coffee. "Let me break the news."

"Of course," Emma chortled. She glanced at her husband, Kahlid, who sat at the end of the table and at her left elbow. "And Kahlid, you keep quiet, too."

"Me?" He held up his hands, feigning surprise. "Why, I'm the soul of secrets, beloved."

"Sometimes," Emma said with a wry laugh.

Ty smiled. He sat across the table from Rachel. She looked incredibly beautiful in her khaki trousers, the soft pink tee, her hair washed and shining like a frame about her face. "I think this can be all sorted out," he soothed.

Kahlid leaned forward and patted Ty's shoulder. "Listen, you two are welcome here any time you can get away. Emma and I know the joy of coming here after being out at these villages. We know we're targets. We know that the Taliban would like to kill us. But being able to come back here..." Kahlid said, gesturing around the room, "...is a slice of heaven on this war-torn earth."

Emma nodded and looked at her cousin. "All you have to do is call Nabi after you fly into Bagram, and he'll pick you up. You're welcome any time, Rachel. The suite wing is yours."

"Thanks," Rachel said, her eyes filling with tears. She sniffed and looked over at Ty. The expression in his eyes told her everything. He loved her.

"Changes are in the air," Kahlid agreed. "Getting to another topic, we had a meeting with Major Klein this morning." He got serious. "Have you heard about a ground arm of Black Jaguar Squadron being created?"

"Yes," Rachel said. "These are women military volunteers who have taken immersion courses in Pashto, gone through a year of paramedic training to be embedded in Marine squads. They're going to put a woman in each squad. She'll then make connection with the women elders of the villages they work with."

"Precisely," Kahlid said. He wiped his mouth with the white linen napkin and picked up his cup of tea. "Colonel Maya Stevenson and her husband, Dane, are flying in tomorrow. The women are already here and getting situated in the BJS tent area."

"Wow, it's moving fast." Rachel whistled.

"You'll both be invited to the meeting tomorrow at 1300."

Ty smiled. "Big changes. Women in ground combat."

"Yes," Emma said with caution, "but they're not there to fight the Taliban as much as make positive connections with the women in the villages. They'll be like a nurse, coming in to take care of the women and children. I think it's a wonderful concept."

Ty frowned. "But there's no guarantee that those Marine forces won't be attacked by Taliban. And if they are, that woman is in that squad and attacked, too."

"Everyone at the Pentagon realizes this," Kahlid agreed. "That's why they've put Colonel Maya Stevens in charge of it. She single-handedly built the all-woman BJS squadron down in Peru and choked off ninety percent of the drug flights out of that country. She's a brilliant tactician, and she's had her vision for this new breed of BJS women all along. These volunteers were also trained at Camp Pendleton, the USMC training base in California, too. They're fully combat qualified."

"Still," Rachel said, "it's a brand new trial for women in combat."

"I think they'll win the hearts and minds of the villagers," Kahlid said. "Women are able to make connections men never will." He grinned over at his red-haired wife.

Chuckling, Emma said, "Bingo!"

Rachel smiled across the table at Ty. She wanted to go to bed with him, hold him, love him until they both were too weak to move. This courageous man had surmounted so much. Tomorrow would come soon enough. They would survive this year, and she knew their love would deepen. She would marry him. And Rachel knew their love would last—forever.

* * * * *

SUSPENSE

Heartstopping stories of intrigue and mystery—
where true love always triumphs.

Harlequin® ROMANTIC SUSPENSE

COMING NEXT MONTH
AVAILABLE FEBRUARY 28, 2012

#1695 OPERATION MIDNIGHT
Cutter's Code
Justine Davis

#1696 A DAUGHTER'S PERFECT SECRET
Perfect, Wyoming
Kimberly Van Meter

#1697 HIGH-STAKES AFFAIR
Stealth Knights
Gail Barrett

#1698 DEADLY RECKONING
Elle James

REQUEST YOUR FREE BOOKS!
2 FREE NOVELS PLUS 2 FREE GIFTS!

ROMANTIC
SUSPENSE

Sparked by Danger, Fueled by Passion.

New York Times *and* USA TODAY *bestselling author Maya Banks presents book three in her miniseries* PREGNANCY & PASSION.

TEMPTED BY HER INNOCENT KISS

Available March 2012 from Harlequin Desire!

There came a time in a man's life when he knew he was well and truly caught. Devon Carter stared down at the diamond ring nestled in velvet and acknowledged that this was one such time. He snapped the lid closed and shoved the box into the breast pocket of his suit.

He had two choices. He could marry Ashley Copeland and fulfill his goal of merging his company with Copeland Hotels, thus creating the largest, most exclusive line of resorts in the world, or he could refuse and lose it all.

Put in that light, there wasn't much he could do except pop the question.

The doorman to his Manhattan high-rise apartment hurried to open the door as Devon strode toward the street. He took a deep breath before ducking into his car, and the driver pulled into traffic.

Tonight was the night. All of his careful wooing, the countless dinners, kisses that started brief and casual and became more breathless—all a lead-up to tonight. Tonight his seduction of Ashley Copeland would be complete, and then he'd ask her to marry him.

He shook his head as the absurdity of the situation hit him for the hundredth time. Personally, he thought William Copeland was crazy for forcing his daughter down Devon's throat.

Ashley was a sweet enough girl, but Devon had no desire

to marry anyone.

William had other plans. He'd told Devon that Ashley had no head for the family business. She was too softhearted, too naive. So he'd made Ashley part of the deal. The catch? Ashley wasn't to know of it. Which meant Devon was stuck playing stupid games.

Ashley was supposed to think this was a grand love match. She was a starry-eyed woman who preferred her animal-rescue foundation over board meetings, charts and financials for Copeland Hotels.

If she ever found out the truth, she wouldn't take it well.

And hell, he couldn't blame her.

But no matter the reason for his proposal, before the night was over, she'd have no doubts that she belonged to him.

What will happen when Devon marries Ashley?
Find out in Maya Banks's passionate new novel
TEMPTED BY HER INNOCENT KISS
Available March 2012 from Harlequin Desire!

Get swept away with author

CATHY GILLEN THACKER

and her new miniseries

Legends of Laramie County

On the Cartwright ranch, it's the women
who endure and run the ranch—and it's time for
lawyer Liz Cartwright to take over. Needing some help
around the ranch, Liz hires Travis Anderson, a fellow
attorney, and Liz's high-school boyfriend. Travis says
he wants to get back to his ranch roots, but Liz knows
Travis is running from something. Old feelings emerge
as they work together, but Liz can't help but wonder
if Travis is home to stay.

Reluctant Texas Rancher

**Available March
wherever books are sold.**

Harlequin *Presents*

USA TODAY bestselling author

Carol Marinelli

begins a daring duet.

THE SECRETS *of* XANOS

Two brothers alike in charisma and power;
separated at birth and seeking revenge…

Nico has always felt like an outsider. He's turned his back on his
parents' fortune to become one of Xanos's most powerful exports
and nothing will stand in his way—until he stumbles
upon a virgin bride….

Zander took his chances on the streets rather than spending another
moment under his cruel father's roof. Now he is unrivaled in
business—and the bedroom! He wants the best people around him,
and Charlotte is the best PA! Can he tempt her
over to the dark side…?

A SHAMEFUL CONSEQUENCE
Available in March

AN INDECENT PROPOSITION
Available in April

www.Harlequin.com

HP13053